Candide

by Scott Hunter

Baker's Plays
7611 Sunset Blvd.
Los Angeles, CA 90042
BAKERSPLAYS.COM

CANDIDE was first performed in November, 2007 by Hesperia High School in Hesperia, California, under the direction of Paula Hunter, with the following casts:

The Black Cast:

In Beautiful Westfalia, Or Thereabouts

CANDIDE, the Optimist . . . . .Jonathan Godinho
CUNEGONDE, the Ingenue . . . . .Nora Hunter
DR. PANGLOSS, the Philosopher .Corey Pickens
PAQUETTE, the Chambermaid. . . . . Tori Johnson
THE OLD WOMAN WITH ONE BUTTOCK . . . . .Nicole Boretz
HEINRICH, the Noble Man . . . . Carey Stark
CACAMBO, the Servant. . . . . .Heather Oliver
BARONESS THUNDER-TEN-TRONCKH. . . . . Brittany Brink
BARON THUNDER-TEN-TRONCKH . . . . .David Smith
VOLTAIRE, the Philosopher. . . . . Josh Vogel
BEN FRANKLIN, the Founding Father. . . . . Troy Al Medina
THE BULGARIAN DESERTER. . . . . .Shelby Young
THE HEAD BULGARIAN SOLDIER. .Josh Lopez
THE BULGARIAN SERGEANT . . . . .Jake Ingram

In Unlucky Portugal

JAMES THE ANABAPTIST . . . . Ian Newsome
THE INSPECTOR GENERAL. . . . . Tommy Leyden
THE GRAND INQUISITOR . . . . Eric King
THE VICEROY OF THE INQUISITION. . . . . .Jaya Singh
THE INEPT EXECUTIONER . . . . Daniel Trombetta
THE OTHER EXECUTIONER, just as inept . . . . Kathryn Haley
THE MAN WHO MARRIED HIS GODMOTHER . . . . Justin Johnson
THE HOT GODMOTHER . . . . O'Brian Padilla
THE MERCHANT WHO HATES BACON. . . . . .Audrey Stretch
DON ISSACHAR, the Happy Person. . . . . .Martin Murphy
THE UNIVERSITY SURGEON. . . . . Rosalia Medrano

In The Port Of Cadiz And Bound For The New World

THE LUCKY NUN . . . . Angela Lapenson
THE UNLUCKY BEGGAR . . . . Britnee Messer
THE DRILL SERGEANT. . . . . O'Brian Padilla
THE FIRST CANNIBAL. . . . . Daniel Trombetta
THE SECOND CANNIBAL . . . . .Justin Johnson
THE THIRD CANNIBAL . . . . Ian Newsome

Across The Ocean In Buenos Ares

DON FERNANDO, the Ladies' Man. . . . . .Zachary Corrales
DON FERNANDO'S FIRST LADY .Melanee Jarboe
DON FERNANDO'S SECOND LADY. . . . . Korionna McKinnon
THE MESSENGER FROM THE JUNGLE . . . . Cerrissa Jo Witte James
THE BUENOS ARES TOWNSWOMAN . . . . Britnee Messer
ANOTHER TOWNSWOMAN. . . . . Shelby Young

Deep In The Jungle Of Paraguay And Even Deeper In El Dorado

THE REVOLUTIONARY COMMANDER . . . . Michaune Borchardt
THE REVOLUTIONARY GUARD . . . . Josh Vogel
THE QUEEN OF THE AMAZON . . . . Kelsey Cole
THE AMAZON PRINCESS . . . . Aimee Pyle
THE OTHER AMAZON PRINCESS . . . . O'Brian Padilla

In The Lawless Port Of Suriname

THE SLAVE AUCTIONEER . . . . Mario Gonzalez
THE SLAVE BIDDER . . . . Alex Nigro
THE PIRATE KING . . . . Troy Al Medina
MARTIN, the Hyper-Active Pessimist . . . . Michael Myers

Among The Wildlife In France

MISS RATTOLI, the French Guide, a Mime . . . . Yesenia Galvez
MADEMOISELLE CLAIRON, a Madame . . . . Audrey Stretch
THE FRENCH INSPECTOR . . . . Joseph Gardner
THE FRENCH IMPOSTOR . . . . Cody McMillan
MADEMOISELLE MIMI . . . . Melanee Jarboe
MADEMOISELLE YOUYOU . . . . Korionna McKinnon

The Freshman Menagerie - Farm Animals, Horses, And Educated Sheep
Rebecca Parra, Jennifer Sakal, Marina Sauchenko, Christa Evans, Eveling
Cerda, Mathew Mejia, Nathan Goff, Crystal Christos, Emily Cutillo, Casey
Carver, Elizabeth Engman, Bryan Estrada, Taylor Stidham

CANDIDE was first performed in November, 2007 by Hesperia High School in Hesperia, California, under the direction of Paula Hunter, with the following casts:

The Gold Cast

In Beautiful Westfalia, Or Thereabouts

CANDIDE, the Optimist . . . . .Quentin Purviance
CUNEGONDE, the Ingenue . . . . Amanda Wilkie
DR. PANGLOSS, the Philosopher . . . . Alex Nigro
PAQUETTE, the Chambermaid . . . . Chelsea Terry
THE OLD WOMAN WITH ONE BUTTOCK . . . . .Khassarah Aflleje
HEINRICH, the Noble Man . . . . Josh Lopez
CACAMBO, the Servant. . . . . Sarita Fowler
BARONESS THUNDER-TEN-TRONCKH. . . . . Esther Ballerteros
BARON THUNDER-TEN-TRONCKH . . . . Brad Bowes
VOLTAIRE, the Philosopher . . . . Josh Vogel
BEN FRANKLIN, the Founding Father. . . . . Bryan Weathers
THE BULGARIAN DESERTER. . . . . .Crystal Leach
THE HEAD BULGARIAN SOLDIER. Carey Stark
THE BULGARIAN SERGEANT . . . . Jeff Rose

In Unlucky Portugal

JAMES THE ANABAPTIST . . . . .Casey Matteson
THE INSPECTOR GENERAL. . . . . Ryan Wade
THE GRAND INQUISITOR . . . . .Michael Myers
THE VICEROY OF THE INQUISITION. . . . . Stacey Spurlock
THE INEPT EXECUTIONER . . . . Paul Lukey
THE OTHER EXECUTIONER, just as inept . . . . Kathryn Haley
THE MAN WHO MARRIED HIS GODMOTHER . . . . Tyler Ferrell
THE HOT GODMOTHER . . . . .Michelle Stites
THE MERCHANT WHO HATES BACON. . . . . Stevi Delich
DON ISSACHAR, the Happy Person. Trace Taft
THE UNIVERSITY SURGEON. . . . . Jessica Vicario

In The Port Of Cadiz And Bound For The New World

THE LUCKY NUN . . . . .Kelsey Cocek
THE UNLUCKY BEGGAR . . . . Britnee Messer
THE DRILL SERGEANT. . . . . .O'Brian Padilla
THE FIRST CANNIBAL. . . . . .Paul Lukey
THE SECOND CANNIBAL . . . . Tyler Ferrell
THE THIRD CANNIBAL. . . . . Casey Matteson

Across The Ocean In Buenos Ares

DON FERNANDO, the Ladies' Man. . . . . .Brandon Bransby
DON FERNANDO'S FIRST LADY .Melanee Jarboe
DON FERNANDO'S SECOND LADY. . . . . Susan Koch
THE MESSENGER FROM THE JUNGLE . . . . Cerrissa Jo Witte James
THE BUENOS ARES TOWNSWOMAN . . . . Britnee Messer
ANOTHER TOWNSWOMAN. . . . . Crystal Leach

Deep In The Jungle Of Paraguay And Even Deeper In
El Dorado
THE REVOLUTIONARY COMMANDER . . . . Michaune Borchardt
THE REVOLUTIONARY GUARD . . . . Josh Vogel
THE QUEEN OF THE AMAZON . . . . Amanda Perkins
THE AMAZON PRINCESS. . . . . .Jessica Guevara
THE OTHER AMAZON PRINCESS .Michelle Stites

In The Lawless Port Of Suriname
THE SLAVE AUCTIONEER. . . . . Ernesto Avaiza
THE SLAVE BIDDER . . . . .Shari Hinson
THE PIRATE KING . . . . .Bryan Weathers
MARTIN, the Hyper-Active Pessimist . . . . .David Smith

Among The Wildlife In France
MISS RATTOLI, the French Guide, a Mime . . . . Alexis Oliva
MADEMOISELLE CLAIRON, a Madame . . . . Amy Cutillo
THE FRENCH INSPECTOR . . . . .Joseph Gardner
THE FRENCH IMPOSTOR . . . . .Jordan Massey
MADEMOISELLE MIMI. . . . . Heather Shrader
MADEMOISELLE YOUYOU . . . . Susan Koch

The Freshman Menagerie - Farm Animals, Horses, And Educated Sheep
Rebecca Parra, Jennifer Sakal, Marina Sauchenko, Christa Evans, Eveling
Cerda, Mathew Mejia, Nathan Goff, Crystal Christos, Emily Cutillo, Casey
Carver, Elizabeth Engman, Bryan Estrada, Taylor Stidham

CHARACTERS

Chapters in which each character appears are in parenthesis:

(Act I prologue = P I, Act II prologue = P II)

In Beautiful Westfalia, Or Thereabouts:

CANDIDE (1, 2, 3, 4, 5, 6, 7, 8, P II, 9, 10, 11, 12, 13, 13½, 14) – The Optimist. Young and handsome - endowed with a most sweet disposition and the most unaffected simplicity, he believes in the Philosophy of Optimism, even in the face of experience. He will not rest until he is reunited with the fair Cunegonde.

CUNEGONDE (1, 2, 5, 6, 7, 8, P II, 9, 11, 12, 13½, 14) – The ingénue. Beautiful and immature, more adventuresome than Candide, she is faithful to Candide unless reasonably large sums of money are involved.

DR. PANGLOSS (P I, 1, 2, 3, 4, 5, 7, 8, 12, 13, 13½, 14) – The Philosopher. Sophisticated, happy and confident, he is the best of all possible teachers. As the play progresses he encounters setback after setback, is riddled with disease, hanged and dissected, yet he steadfastly clings to his Philosophy of Optimism.

PAQUETTE (P I, 1, 2, 3, 5, 6, 7, 8, P II, 9, 10, 11, 12, 13, 13½, 14) – Cunegonde's chambermaid. She is the dark lady to Cunegonde's fair youth. She is beautiful and worldly. No man is safe around her with the notable exception of the unwavering Candide.

THE OLD WOMAN WITH NO NAME AND ONLY ONE BUTTOCK (P I, 1, 2, 5, 6, 7, 8, P II, 9, 11, 12, 13, 13½, 14) – Cunegonde's other servant. The daughter of a Pope, she was once a beautiful princess who is now old and ugly and left by cannibals with only one buttock. She is very opinionated and seeks to dominate.

CACAMBO (1, 2, 3, 4, 5, 6, 7, 8, P II, 9, 10, 11, 12, 13, 13½, 14) – Candide's trusty servant. Cacambo is a woman dressed as a man in a thinly veiled attempt to create more women's parts. She would secretly like to be more than a servant to Candide.

HEINRICH (1, 2, 10, 12, 13, 13½, 14) – Heir to the Castle Thunder-ten-tronckh and brother to Cunegonde. He believes he is the best of all possible humans. He defends his notion of nobility and refuses to allow Cunegonde to marry below her station in life, even when she is reduced to a scullery maid.

BARONESS THUNDER-TEN-TRONCKH (P I, 1, 2) - Not so beautiful as she thinks she is. She dies, after prolonged staggering, when the Bulgarians attack.

BARON THUNDER-TEN-TRONCKH (P I, 1, 2) - One of the most powerful men in Europe. So enlightened, he provides an education for all his subjects, even the farm animals. He dies while narrating when the Bulgarians attack.

VOLTAIRE (P I)- The Great Philosopher. He dies in the prologue rather than stick around to see how we've adapted his work.

BEN FRANKLIN (P I)- The Founding Father. His purpose in this play is to explain that it is unpatriotic to complain about Voltaire's somewhat naughty sense of humor.

SHEEP (P I, 1, 2, 3, 8, P II, 11, 12, 13, 13½, 14) – Four or more educated sheep (not all Sheep will appear in each listed scene). They wear ribbons in their hair, Pink for girls, blue for boys.

HORSES (1, 2, 7, 8, P II, 9, 11) - Two horses. They play native cannibals in a scene deleted for time and then restored by popular demand.

In Bulgaria:

THE ARMY DESERTER (2) - AWOL from the Bulgarian Army. He runs away rather than march. He leaves behind an empty uniform in Candide's size.

BULGARIAN SOLDIER 1 (P I, 2, 3) - The Head of the Bulgarian Army. He dies in the battle of Westphalia but doesn't stop talking.

BULGARIAN SOLDIER 2 (P I, 2) - The Bulgarian Captain. A master at the Bulgarian Drill. He helps conscript Candide into the army.

CHRISTOPHER COLUMBUS (3) - He passes on his discoveries from the new world to others. He takes part in the joke most likely to be cut.

In Unlucky Portugal:

JAMES THE ANABAPTIST (P I, 4) - Would-be narrator. He dies in a shipwreck because he is too good to be allowed to keep living.

THE INSPECTOR GENERAL (5, 7, 9, 11, 14) - Of the Portuguese Inquisition. He will never rest until he gets his man. Never … never.

THE GRAND INQUISITOR (P I, 5, 6, 7, 14) - The head of the Portuguese Church. A pious man, he dresses up in a tutu to visit his mistress, Cunegonde. He dies at the hand of Candide.

THE VICEROY OF THE INQUISITION (5, 6, 7, 9, 11, 14) - The chief clerk to the Grand Inquisitor. She (we assume you've run out of boys by now to play this part) joins forces with the Inspector General to track down Candide. She would rather rest, but never gets a chance.

THE FIRST EXECUTIONER (P I, 5, 7, 14)- Not as good at killing as one might think from his name.

THE SECOND EXECUTIONER(P I, 5, 7) – Just as inept as the first executioner.

A BISCAYAN WHO MARRIED HIS GODMOTHER (5) - Hot for his Godmother, and then just plain hot. Put to death by fire at the Auto-da-fe. Apparently it's illegal to marry your Godmother. Who knew?

THE GODMOTHER (5) - Still very young and very hot; too hot to be put to death, even by fire.

THE MERCHANT WHO HATES BACON (5) - burned alive for not liking bacon. Who knew?

DON ISSACHAR (P I, 6, 7, 14) - The Banker. He bestows expensive gifts on Cunegonde because she seems so grateful. He is killed in a duel with Candide and dies for love.

FLASHBACK CUNEGONDE (6, 13½,)- She appears whenever Cunegonde replays a flashback. She need not look at all like Cunegonde, or be a woman for that matter, and wears a sign around her neck to indicate her part.

FLASHBACK BULGARIAN CAPTAIN (6) - Flashback version of the real character. Could be played by the real character with a proper sign. He forces Cunegonde to do housekeeping against her will.

FLASHBACK GRAND INQUISITOR (6) - Flashback version of the real character. Could be played by the real character with a proper sign.

FLASHBACK DON ISSACHAR (6) –Flashback version of the real character. Could be played by the real character with a proper sign.

FLASHBACK BARON (6) - Flashback version of the real character. Could be played by the real character with a proper sign.

FLASHBACK HEINRICH (6) - Flashback version of the real character. Could be played by the real character with a proper sign.

The Road to Spain and on to Sea:

THE UNIVERSITY SURGEON (7) - Buys the body of Dr. Pangloss for the purposes of dissection. Dissects with a butcher knife because a scalpel is too small to be seen by the audience, besides, it's funnier.

THE LUCKY NUN (7) - Finds a box of jewels and breaks her vows of silence.

THE UNLUCKY BEGGAR (7) - Doesn't find jewels but gets a crust of bread.

THE DRILL SERGEANT(7, 8, 9) - Hires Candide's entourage to fight in South America after watching them march like Bulgarians.

FLASHBACK OLD WOMAN (8) - Not up to the task, she's quickly replaced by the real Old Woman who insists on self-flashbacking.

THE FIRST CANNIBAL (P II) - Turns to cannibalism when all else fails.

THE SECOND CANNIBAL (P II) - Has a taste for rump roast.

THE THIRD CANNIBAL (P II) - Just as hungry as the other two.

THE EUNUCH (P II) - An unhappy Eunuch. Probably unhappy because he only has one line.

In Argentina:

DON FERNANDO D'IBARAA Y FIGUEORA Y MASCARENES Y LAMPOUR-DOS Y SOUZA (P I, 9, 11, 14) - The Ladies' Man. He has his eye on Cunegonde and the power to take what he wants.

DON FERNANDO'S FIRST LADY (9) - Sexy. She is not enough for Don Fernando

DON FERNANDO'S SECOND LADY (9) - Sexy. Two is not enough.

THE MESSENGER FROM THE JUNGLE (9) - Delivers bad news to Don Fernando, and pays for it in the end.

In Paraguay:

THE REVOLUTIONARY COMMANDER (10) - Protects the Jungle for the fighting friar of Paraguay.

THE REVOLUTIONARY COMRADE (10) - skilled at dance as well as weaponry.

In El Dorado:

THE QUEEN OF THE AMAZON (P I, 11, 14) - Is queen in El Dorado, where all women are queens.

THE AMAZON PRINCESS (11) - Thinks gold is dirt.

THE OTHER AMAZON PRINCESS (11) – Thinks dirt is gold.

In Suriname:

THE SLAVE AUCTIONEER (12) - Auctions Pangloss and Heinrich to a pirate.

THE SLAVE BIDDER (12) - Drops out of the bidding after inspecting the merchandise.

THE PIRATE KING (P I, 12, 13, 14) - Buys Pangloss and Heinrich as galley slaves - steals Candide's fortune, only to die at sea.

MARTIN, THE PESSIMIST (12, 13, 13½, 14) - Servant to Candide. Robbed by his wife, beaten by his son, forsaken by his daughter, he believes nothing will ever be for the best. He presents his case in the most hyper-anxious, abrasive, and animated way possible. Usually he's right. He refuses to accept that he is a supporting character. He dies rather than become happy.

In France:

MISS RATTOLI (13½) - the French Guide. She is the most detestable of all creatures - a mime.

MADEMOISELLE CLAIRON (P I, 13½, 14) - the Madame - A business woman, she relieves Candide of his fortune.

POLICEMAN 1 (13½) - The French Impostor - He pretends to be Cunegonde to lure Candide toward ruin.

POLICEMAN 2 (13½) - The French Inspector - He is in the corrupt service of Mademoiselle Clairon.

MADEMOISELLE MIMI (13½) - In the employment of the Madame.

MADEMOISELLE YOUYOU (13½) - Discusses philosophy with Pangloss.

FLASHBACK CACAMBO (13½) - Flashback version of the real character. Could be played by the real character with a proper sign.

FLASHBACK DON FERNANDO (13½) - Flashback version of the real character. Could be played by the real character with a proper sign.

SETTING

A unit set, with playing areas on different levels. The many scene changes can be accomplished with the addition of small furniture pieces, a rolling platform or, in most situations, narration. Behind the platforms is a scrim suitable for projections and silhouettes.

AUTHOR'S NOTE

I originally adapted *Candide* because we wanted to have a play with enough parts for all our actors. *Candide* worked out well, with more female leads than male leads and plenty of intermediate roles. A convenient line in the prologue warned the audience to suspend their disbelief since some of our young women would need to play men, and many of our actors would be playing more than one part. Even our freshmen, usually an underserved population, were eager to play the farm animals.

Having a play big enough for all our actors caused two problems. First, it was big enough for all our actors. We had to make sure that we kept a brisk pace and didn't spend even a nanosecond on set changes. Our solution was to use a unit set and project images onto a scrim. This was cheap (how much does a PowerPoint cost?) and effective. There can be many other solutions to the scene change problem, but the directions written in the play reflect what worked for us.

The second problem was *Candide's* somewhat risqué content. We were afraid of getting complaints. We did *Oklahoma* the year before and got complaints (oh, that Ado Annie). We did *Peter Pan* and got complaints (it was the tights). We decided to take a proactive course. First we made it known that *Candide* was on our state's approved reading list. Secondly, we wrote an introduction that seemed to say it was unpatriotic to complain about the great Voltaire. But we went one step further and put a disclaimer on the poster which read:

THIS PLAY HAS BEEN RATED

PG	PARENTAL GUIDANCE SUGGESTED
SOME MATERIAL MAY NOT BE SUITABLE FOR CHILDREN	

FOR
CV – CARTOON VIOLENCE
SA – SWASHBUCKLING ACTION
AC – ADULT CONTENT
BN – BRIEF NUDITY
AND
S – SHEEP

Of course, there was no brief nudity, which was the only complaint we got.

ACT I

Prologue

(AT RISE: The stage is empty. A slide show begins. The images are a brief preview of what lies ahead: slides overlapping and flowing briskly across the scrim, period etchings and woodcuts depicting life in the 18th century. There are battles, pirates, Auto da Fe, the earthquake of Lisbon [1755], slavery in South America, El Dorado, Paris and pastoral life, jumbled together in a fast paced bombardment set to heroic music.)

(As the slice show ends, we hear laughter and watch as **PANGLOSS** *and* **PAQUETTE,** *their shadows silhouetted on the scrim, play a flirtatious game of cat and mouse.* **PANGLOSS** *tickles her and chases her out of view as the* **BARON** *and* **BARONESS** *enter opposite.)*

BARON. Ladies and Gentlemen, may I present your narrators for this evening.

(He points to the wings. No one enters. The shadows chase back onto the scrim and we hear more laughter. **PANGLOSS** *chases* **PAQUETTE** *around the scrim and onto the stage. They freeze when they see the audience and quickly reshevel.)*

*(***PAQUETTE** *is young and sultry and it can be assumed that most every man in the cast,* **CANDIDE** *being the notable exception, covets some experience with her by the way they change their behavior when she's around.* **PANGLOSS** *is the most dignified man imaginable, perfectly groomed and content with himself.)*

BARONESS. And now tonight's narrators.

BARON. One of the most generous women in all Europe, Paquette, the chambermaid.

PAQUETTE. Guten Tag.

BARONESS. With her is Doctor Pangloss, philosopher and teacher.

PANGLOSS. Good evening, Ladies and Gentlemen. By a show of hands, how many of you are here for the intellectual stimulation of exploring the mind of the greatest philosopher of the eighteenth century, Voltaire? A man who once said, "To hold a pen, is to be at war."

(No one raises their hand.)

None of you?

(The **OLD WOMAN** *enters. She walks with a waddle in her gate due to her large but imbalanced buttock, which she enjoys emphasizing with a pose or a bend.)*

OLD WOMAN. By show of hands, how many are here for the senseless violence and brief nudity?

(wild applause from the audience)

I thought so.

PAQUETTE. *(with great disdain for the* **OLD WOMAN***)* Our other partner in narration.

OLD WOMAN. *(to* **PAQUETTE***, with equal cattiness)* Started without me?

(to audience)

Good evening. I am The Old Woman with No Name and Only One Buttock. You're probably wondering why I have only one buttock, well, I'll tell you –

PAQUETTE. Some other time. This is the rest of our cast. The Westphalia Community Players.

(The rest of the **CAST** *runs on stage, striking exaggerated poses.)*

PANGLOSS. Tonight's play is, "The Westphalia Community Players Present *Candide*." It is not Voltaire's *Candide*. That's something entirely different.

PAQUETTE. Voltaire's *Candide* is a picaresque novel about a young man who finds himself optimistically living in the best of all possible worlds.

PANGLOSS. It spans four continents, and eleven countries.

PAQUETTE. It features over a hundred characters and takes place over many years.

OLD WOMAN. The Westphalia Community Players' *Candide* includes all those things, too…, and a lot of overacting.

PANGLOSS. To accomplish our goal, some of the players will have to take on more than one part, and some of our women will need to play men. Please bear with us. Now, let's have a moment of silence for Voltaire.

(The CAST *unfreezes for a moment of silence.)*

OLD WOMAN. Now let's go butcher him.

(The CAST *cheers and re-freezes.)*

PANGLOSS. Voltaire is barely remembered these days. Yet, it was the words of Voltaire that inspired a young Thomas Jefferson, a George Washington, and our other founding fathers. In fact, when Benjamin Franklin went to Paris as ambassador of the First Continental Congress, whom did he seek out? Voltaire! They met in the spring of 1778, while our colonies still fought for independence. The meeting may have gone something like this.

(Two cast members step forward. They wear signs around their neck that read **VOLTAIRE** *and* **FRANKLIN**.*)*

VOLTAIRE. Ben!

FRANKLIN. Vol.

PANGLOSS. You see, they were on a first syllable basis.

VOLTAIRE. How's the revolution?

FRANKLIN. Win some, lose some.

VOLTAIRE. That's revolution.

FRANKLIN. How're you feeling these days?

VOLTAIRE. I suffer from lumbago.

FRANKLIN. Sorry.

VOLTAIRE. And sudden death.

> (**VOLTAIRE** *falls over dead. Others drag him away.*)

PANGLOSS. Sadly, Voltaire died before he could see our revolution succeed, but when you tuck yourself in at night, in the safety and security of a free, democratic nation, pay homage to one of those few who invented the idea, the great Voltaire.

ALL. *(cheering)* Voltaire!

PANGLOSS. And if you feel at all like complaining to our Board Members about the somewhat naughty content of tonight's show remember, it's not us. Oh, no. It's the *great* Voltaire.

ALL. *(knowingly)* Voltaire.

PANGLOSS. Now, we must get on with our story.

OLD WOMAN. We got to vacate by 9:30 to allow the custodial crew time to clean up.

PANGLOSS. In the interim, let me assure you that tonight, on this stage, you will see –

BULGARIAN SOLDIERS. War –

DON FERNANDO. Love –

PIRATE. Pirates –

QUEEN. Riches, beyond the comprehension of mortal man –

EXECUTIONER 1. Death by fire –

EXECUTIONER 2. Hanging –

DON ISSACAR. And impalement –

GRAND INQUISITOR. Inquisitions –

MADAME. Brothels –

SHEEP 1. And sheep…Lots of sheep…

> (*The* **SHEEP** *gets back down on all fours.*)

I mean…baaaaa.

PANGLOSS. And at the end of the evening, I will tell you the meaning of life. Yes, you will learn, on this stage, the answer to the age old question, "Why?"

ALL. Pourquoi?

PAQUETTE. And now, The Westphalia Community Players Present *Candide.*

OLD WOMAN. We take you now to Westphalia, the place, not the Volkswagen.

Scene One

(All exit except for the NARRATORS, BARON, BARON-ESS. A slide appears on the scrim: a picture of a castle accompanied by the words, "Chapter One: How Candide Was Brought Up in a Magnificent Castle, and How He Was Driven Thence.")

PANGLOSS. Chapter 1: How Candide was brought up in a magnificent castle, and how he was driven thence. Enter Baron Thunder-ten-tronckh.

PAQUETTE. One of the most powerful lords of the realm.

BARON. *(flirting)* And with one of the longest names.

BARONESS. *(interrupting)* And his wife, the Baroness.

BARON. We have the most beautiful castle in all of Europe.

BARONESS. Servants, serfs, and livestock, obey our every whim.

BARON. And when we tell a joke everyone laughs.

(The NARRATORS laugh.)

BARONESS. This is indeed, perfection.

BARON. And yet...

BARONESS. And yet...

BARON. Something is missing. But what?

(A BABY flies in, tossed high in the air from the wings. The BARONESS catches it.)

BARON. An heir. Of course. What shall we call him?

BARONESS. Something short that goes with Thunder-ten-tronckh.

BARON. We shall call him Heinrich.

BARONESS. Oh, I like the "Rich" part.

(A second BABY flies in and the BARONESS nimbly catches it in her other hand. This BABY is wrapped in pink.)

BARON. It's a girl. One of each.

BARONESS. How in balance the universe is.

BARON. We shall call her…Cunegonde.

BARONESS. Say what?

(A **THIRD BABY** *flies in. It overflies its mark and bounces to a stop on the floor. The* **BARON** *and* **BARONESS** *stand over it, curious.)*

BARON. It's not mine.

BARONESS. Mine, neither!

PANGLOSS. Indeed, it was the illegitimate son of the Baron's sister,

OLD WOMAN. She refused to marry the gentleman because he could *only* trace his family tree back through eleven generations of nobility.

BARON. We will raise this child as our own, for he is the slight imperfection,

BARONESS. That proves how close to perfect we are.

BARON. We shall call him…

BOTH. Candide.

PANGLOSS. We now jump ahead many years to about 1750.

*(***PANGLOSS** *takes the* **BABIES** *and throws them offstage.)*

The boy Candide is nearly a man.

*(***CANDIDE** *enters carrying an apple.* **CACAMBO**, *his trusty servant, follows. All others exit.* **CANDIDE** *is handsome, wide-eyed and green.* **CACAMBO** *is a woman dressed as a man, a fact lost on* **CANDIDE**.*)*

CANDIDE. Cacambo.

CACAMBO. Yes, master.

CANDIDE. Look at this. An apple. Like that first apple in the garden of Eden. Describe what you see.

*(***CANDIDE** *throws the apple straight up into the air. It comes down with a splat.* **CACAMBO** *cleans up the apple.)*

CACAMBO. The apple was thrown. The apple fell. Now it's mush.

CANDIDE. Did you ever wonder why the apple doesn't fall to the side or straight up, for that matter.

(**CANDIDE** *takes the apple and throws it again, this time higher.*)

CACAMBO. No.

CANDIDE. Well, you are in luck, because Sir Isaac Newton did.

CACAMBO. Beg pardon, Master, but I'd bet the apples fell the same way before Newton sat under that tree.

CANDIDE. Not so. Without a law, nature was unpredictable.

(**CANDIDE** *takes the apple and throws it even higher.* **CACAMBO** *faithfully cleans up.*)

CACAMBO. But that still doesn't help me clean up the mess, does it? Are we going to do this all day?

CANDIDE. Yes.

(**CANDIDE** *throws the apple again.* **CUNEGONDE,** *enters opposite, followed by her servant* **PAQUETTE. CUNE-GONDE** *is the beautiful paragon of immaturity.*)

PAQUETTE. Enter Cunegonde, seventeen years of age, red-cheeked and desirable.

CUNEGONDE. You think?

PAQUETTE. It's not my place to think, my lady. It's my place to serve.

CUNEGONDE. Paquette, don't call me "my lady." It sounds so old fashioned. Call me, "Oh, Enlightened One."

PAQUETTE. I'll try to remember.

CUNEGONDE. This is the age of enlightenment, after all, when even a girl can get an education. Every day I learn some new lesson. Yesterday, I learned why the sky is blue.

PAQUETTE. Why?

CUNEGONDE. I forget, but there's a reason for it, and isn't that comforting. There's a reason for everything. Cause and effect. I want to know why the flowers are red and...

(*She freezes when she sees* **CANDIDE**. *She involuntarily slinks to the floor and strikes a seductive pose.*)

CUNEGONDE. *(cont.)* Paquette, do you see Candide over there?

PAQUETTE. Um…Yes.

CUNEGONDE. Is he looking at me?

PAQUETTE. No.

CUNEGONDE. Why isn't he looking at me?

PAQUETTE. He appears to be engrossed in one of his usual activities.

*(*CANDIDE *throws up the apple. It lands in the audience.* CACAMBO *climbs down off the stage to fetch it.)*

CUNEGONDE. Paquette, since you are older than I, and being a peasant you are, by definition, more worldly, perhaps you can advise me in this area. Do you think him handsome?

(The OLD WOMAN *enters talking.)*

OLD WOMAN. *(ominously)* Be careful… Be careful…

(She poses and waits to be introduced. No one introduces her.)

Never mind. I'll introduce myself. Enter Cunegonde's nurse, the Old Woman with No Name and Only One Buttock –

PAQUETTE. But that's a different story.

OLD WOMAN. Be careful, Cunegonde.

CUNEGONDE. You are old, Old Woman, and you can't possibly understand what we are talking about.

OLD WOMAN. Try me.

CUNEGONDE. Love.

OLD WOMAN. Love? Believe me, my girl, it isn't "love." Men are interested in only one thing, and it isn't love.

CUNEGONDE. Well, I know that. Men are single minded in their pursuit of spiritual peace through the metaphysical rejection of the physical world. But I am only a woman, and therefore, when I look at Candide, my heart beats, my mouth waters, and my fingers get all tingly.

PAQUETTE. So do mine.

CUNEGONDE. When *I* look at Candide, *your* fingers get all tingly? How very strange.

(*Enter* **HEINRICH**. *He is handsome...in his own mind.*)

OLD WOMAN. Enter Heinrich, heir to the Thunder-ten-tronckh Estate. Also known as Rich.

PAQUETTE. Also known as Heinie.

HEINRICH. In this age of science, we need no magic mirrors to tell us who's the fairest of them all. An ordinary mirror will do.

(*He pulls out a mirror and examines all parts of himself.*)

Yes you are. Oh, yes you are. Um...like cotton candy. See? Enlighten that. Cause and effect...

(*He notices* **PAQUETTE** *watching him. He's suddenly tongue-tied.*)

Paquette....? You are loo...loo...looking well, this morning.

PAQUETTE. Am I, Heinie? Looking well?

HEINRICH. Shh. Don't call me Heinie...You...ah...I...must pee.

(*He runs out.* **PANGLOSS** *enters with the* **BARON, BARONESS,** *and* **SHEEP**. *The* **SHEEP** *wear ribbons in their hair to identify their sex, pink for girl, blue for boy.*)

BARONESS. Enter Doctor Pangloss, the fore-mentioned, foremost philosopher and teacher of our time.

BARON. Being the most progressive Baron in all Europe, every day at castle Thunder-ten-tronckh begins with lessons.

BARONESS. Even for the servants.

OLD WOMAN. Even for the farm animals.

PANGLOSS. I can prove that there is no effect without a cause, that this is the best of all possible worlds, that the Baron's castle is the best of all possible castles, and our Lady, the best of all possible Baronesses.

BARONESS. A man of enormous intellect.

PANGLOSS. Gather around students.

HEINRICH. That Heinrich is not the handsomest of all possible men....

(There is no response from anyone.)

...proceed.

PANGLOSS. But the world, being the *only* world, *must* be the best of all possible worlds.

PAQUETTE. But –

PANGLOSS. Recess!

*(Everyone runs out except **PAQUETTE** and **PANGLOSS**. Two **SHEEP** shake their heads as they exit slowly.)*

SHEEP 1. And that's why you don't educate the serving class.

SHEEP 2. She's new, give her a chance.

PANGLOSS. Paquette, perhaps philosophy is not your strong subject. Perhaps you are better suited for some other study. Physics? Newton's third law motion.

PAQUETTE. What does Newton's third law concern?

PANGLOSS. The attraction of heavenly bodies.

*(They laugh flirtatiously as **PANGLOSS** blocks her exit. **PANGLOSS** chases **PAQUETTE** off. Their silhouettes appear on the scrim. The **BARONESS, BARON** and **CUNEGONDE** enter.)*

BARONESS. Next came the moment that would change the lives of our protagonists forever.

BARON. After class Miss Cunegonde saw, through the bushes, Doctor Pangloss giving a lecture in experimental philosophy to the chambermaid, Paquette.

BARONESS. As Miss Cunegonde had a great disposition for the sciences, she watched intently.

*(**PANGLOSS** catches **PAQUETTE**, and they engage in an exaggerated game of patty-cake.)*

BARON. Then she ran to fetch Candide.

*(**CUNEGONDE** pulls **CANDIDE** on from the wings.)*

CUNEGONDE. Observe with the utmost attention the experiment which is repeated before our eyes.

CANDIDE. I don't think that's Newton's Third Law. Newton's third law states that for every action there is an equal and opposite reaction, and...

(CUNEGONDE *drops her handkerchief.*)

BARON. Action: The lady dropped her handkerchief.

BARONESS. Reaction: the young man picked it up.

BARON. She innocently took hold of his hand.

BARONESS. And he, as innocently, kissed hers.

BARON. Their eyes sparkled.

BARONESS. Their knees trembled.

BARON. Their hands...strayed.

(*Like proud parents, they watch* CANDIDE *and* CUNEGONDE *play patty-cake: high-five patty-cakes, round the world patty-cakes, behind the back patty-cakes.* HEINRICH *enters and watches curiously.*)

HEINRICH. What's Candide doing to sister?

(*The* BARON *and* BARONESS *snap out of their trance and rush to separate the twosome.*)

BARON. Behold! Cause and effect. I salute you, Candide... with my foot!

(*He kicks* CANDIDE *in the buttock. They drag away* CUNEGONDE, *reaching and crying. The* BARON *returns briefly to throw* CANDIDE's *suitcases at him.* CACAMBO *brings in* CANDIDE's *worldly possessions. They pack as they talk. The worldly possessions include only useless pop-culture items designed to get a cheap laugh just because* CANDIDE *owns them, such as Star Wars action figures or celebrity posters.*)

CANDIDE. Where will we go, Cacambo?

CACAMBO. We?

CANDIDE. We have only ever lived in this, the best of all possible worlds.

CACAMBO. We?

CANDIDE. We will leave behind this wealth and happiness.

CACAMBO. We? Master, technically, I am employed by the Baron.

CANDIDE. Surely you don't expect a gentle soul in my position to travel without a serving man.

CACAMBO. What position is that?

CANDIDE. Homeless and poor.

CACAMBO. Cheer up, master. From my limited experience, it's still very clear, things could get worse.

*(**CANDIDE** piles up his suitcases onto **CACAMBO** to carry. One by one they load him down until **CACAMBO** staggers with every step.)*

Scene Two

(Slide: a picture of war accompanied by the words, "Chapter Two: How Things Got Worse." *The* NAR-RATORS *enter.)*

OLD WOMAN. Chapter Two: How things got worse.

PANGLOSS. Candide, thus driven out of paradise, rambled a long time without knowing where he went.

PAQUETTE. Sometimes he raised his eyes, all bedewed with tears, towards the magnificent castle, where dwelt the fairest of young baronesses.

(CACAMBO collapses from the weight of the suitcases. Out cold. CANDIDE doesn't notice.)

PANGLOSS. And he made a vow, there and then, the kind of singular vow that gives a man strength through any adventure and any adversity.

CANDIDE. Oh, Cunegonde, now that I know what love is, I vow to never rest until we are reunited.

(CANDIDE hurls himself onto the ground, sobbing. The NARRATORS exit. An ARMY DESERTER sprints in opposite and stops, out of breath. He hears voices offstage, voices with strange Bulgarian accents.)

BULGARIAN SOLDIER 1. *(offstage)* He went that way!

BULGARIAN SOLDIER 2. *(offstage)* Stop, you insolent deserter! Stop we say!

(The ARMY DESERTER strips off his uniform coat, panics, and runs out into the audience to hide among the rows. The BULGARIAN SOLDIERS run on and skid to a stop when they get to the edge of the stage, apparently too afraid of the drop to follow. They call after the hidden figure.)

BULGARIAN SOLDIER 2. Run you filthy coward!

BULGARIAN SOLDIER 1. I salute you with a rude foreign hand gesture.

(BULGARIAN SOLDIER 2 grabs up the ARMY DESERT-ER's uniform coat and starts to throw it into the audience in disgust.)

BULGARIAN SOLDIER 2. I hurl poo at your fleeing backside like an angry circus monkey.

(A wallet falls out of the uniform, The **BULGARIAN SOLDIERS** *pounce on it. No money, though.)*

BULGARIAN SOLDIER 1. We draw a mustache on the wallet sized picture of your mother.

BULGARIAN SOLDIER 2. Nevermind. She already has one!

(The **ARMY DESERTER** *stands up in the audience and points at the* **BULGARIAN SOLDIERS***.)*

ARMY DESERTER. Hey!

(The **BULGARIAN SOLDIERS** *draw guns and shoot at the* **ARMY DESERTER** *who zig-zags out the back.)*

BULGARIAN SOLDIER 2. Hold still, you illegitimate son of an unguent emollient.

BULGARIAN SOLDIER 1. What does that mean, exactly?

BULGARIAN SOLDIER 2. I do not know.

BULGARIAN SOLDIER 1. We have the uniform. Perhaps that's enough insults for now.

BULGARIAN SOLDIER 2. Oh, well, conscripts just don't respond to insults the way they used to.

BULGARIAN SOLDIER 1. It's always, "Oh, everybody is equal," and "I've got free will," and –

*(***BULGARIAN SOLDIER 1** *spies* **CANDIDE***'s prone figure.)*

Hello.

BULGARIAN SOLDIER 2. What?

BULGARIAN SOLDIER 1. Faith, comrade, yonder is a well made young fellow.

(He holds up the discarded uniform, estimating its size.)

And about the right size.

(They approach **CANDIDE** *and startle him.)*

Please sir, will you dine with us?

CANDIDE. You do me much honor, but I have no money.

BULGARIAN SOLDIER 2. Money, sir!

BULGARIAN SOLDIER 1. Men were born to assist one another.

CANDIDE. This is precisely the doctrine of Master Pangloss; and I am convinced, everything is for the best.

BULGARIAN SOLDIER 2. Oh, it is. It is.

(They wrestle **CANDIDE** *into the uniform, beating him when he resists. The* **NARRATORS** *pop out while the struggle unfolds.)*

PAQUETTE. So saying, they handcuffed him, and carried him away to join the Bulgarian Army.

PANGLOSS. There he was made to march, to wheel about to the right, to the left, and they gave him thirty blows with a cane.

OLD WOMAN. The next day he performed his marching exercises a little better, and they gave him only twenty.

(The **NARRATORS** *exit. The* **SOLDIERS** *release* **CAN-DIDE**, *now fully uniformed, and exit laughing.* **CANDIDE** *revives* **CACAMBO**.)*

CANDIDE. Cacambo. Wake up. It's me.

CACAMBO. Candide?

CANDIDE. Yes.

CACAMBO. Look at you. In uniform and everything.

CANDIDE. I've joined the Bulgarian Army.

CACAMBO. The Bulgarians? They're especially ruthless.

CANDIDE. I don't think so. Mostly we just practice marching. Sergeant says, the Bulgarian marching is so intimidating, we won't even have to fight. We call it, "The Bulgarian Drill."

(Enter the **BULGARIAN ARMY**. *The two* **BULGARIAN SOLDIERS** *climb the platform and call their army to order.)*

BULGARIAN SOLDIER 1. Gentlemen, the time has come to go to war.

(The **SOLDIERS** *cheer.)*

BULGARIAN SOLDIER 2. At the end of this day, fifty percent of you will lie dead in pools of blood, dismembered on the battle field.

(The **SOLDIERS** *cheer less enthusiastically.)*

BULGARIAN SOLDIER 1. Twenty-five percent will die instantaneously with no dismemberment at all.

BULGARIAN SOLDIER 2. But the important thing to remember is, there is no shame in that.

BULGARIAN SOLDIER 2. Some of you, the fortunate fifteen percent, will suffer unbearably painful dismemberment, but not die.

BULGARIAN SOLDIER 1. Seventy-five percent of the fifteen percent will go on to rewarding careers in the panhandling industry.

BULGARIAN SOLDIER 1. Ten percent will not die.

BULGARIAN SOLDIER 2. Or suffer dismemberment

BULGARIAN SOLDIER 1. But will endure emotional scars and face years of expensive therapy.

BULGARIAN SOLDIER 2. The rest of you will come through unscathed.

(The **SOLDIERS** *cheer.)*

BULGARIAN SOLDIER 1. So let's begin, the Bulgarian Drill!

CANDIDE. Wait. Sir, who are we fighting against?

BULGARIAN SOLDIER 2. Does it matter?

CANDIDE. It matters to me.

BULGARIAN SOLDIER 1. And, who are you, private?

CANDIDE. One of what we all are, a man of free will.

BULGARIAN SOLDIER 2. Oh, very well, what is this? Tuesday?

(He pulls out a schedule of events.)

Tuesday we march against a small country called… Westphalia.

CANDIDE. That can't be.

BULGARIAN SOLDIER 1. Certainly it can. Says so right there. Westphalia.

BULGARIAN SOLDIER 2. *(reading from schedule)* One day for overthrow. Two days for pillaging. 30,000 casualties.

BULGARIAN SOLDIER 1. We'll be home for the weekend.

CANDIDE. Westphalia is peaceful. Please. Westphalia is the home of Cunegonde, the paragon of womankind.

BULGARIAN SOLDIER 1. Is she beautiful?

CANDIDE. Helen of Troy is plain by comparison.

BULGARIAN SOLDIER 1. Is she pure?

CANDIDE. Her virtue is unchallenged.

BULGARIAN SOLDIER 1. Dibs on Cunegonde!

ALL SOLDIERS. Dibs on Cunegonde, I called her first. etc.

(All argue. Heroic music starts, the music for the Bulgarian Drill. The arguers immediately freeze.)

BULGARIAN SOLDIER 2. Forward! For the Bulgarian Drill!

(They do the Bulgarian Drill which turns out to be very much like a cross between the Macarena and the Three Amigos salute. The **WESTPHALIANS** *and* **SHEEP** *rush out and take menacing poses that interrupt the marching.)*

PAQUETTE. Just then, fearing a pre-emptive attack that would leave them all massacred, Westphalia attacked...

OLD WOMAN. And all were massacred.

BARON. Attack.

(A fierce war breaks out.)

During the battle, the brave Baron Thunde-ten-tronckh –

(The **BULGARIAN SOLDIER 2** *sneaks up behind the* **BARON** *and slices the* **BARON***'s throat.)*

BULGARIAN SOLDIER 2. Was killed while distracted.

HEINRICH. Heinrich, despite a valiant defensive strategy...,

*(***HEINRICH** *pulls the* **SHEEP** *in front of him as shields. They die one by one until* **HEINRICH** *is alone.)*

...was eventually cornered and forced to surrender his life.

Scene Three

(Slide: A picture of dead bodies on a battlefield accompanied by the words, "Chapter Three: How Candide Escaped from the Bulgarians and What Befell Him afterward." **PANGLOSS** *pops up to narrate.)*

PANGLOSS. Chapter 3: How Candide escaped from the Bulgarians and what befell him afterward.

*(**PANGLOSS** exits. **CANDIDE** and **CACAMBO** sneak out from hiding and examine all the dead bodies and severed limbs.)*

CANDIDE. Cacambo, an hour ago these men were laughing and shouting orders.

*(**CANDIDE** picks up the head of **BULGARIAN SOLDIER 1**.)*

Alas, poor whatever-your-name-was! I knew him, Cacambo; a fellow of infinite jest…Here hung those lips that I have kissed I know not how oft.

CACAMBO. Pardon?

CANDIDE. Hamlet. Act 5, scene 1.

*(**CANDIDE** sees **CUNEGONDE**'s bloody handkerchief. He tosses the **BULGARIAN**'s severed head to **CACAMBO**. **CACAMBO** juggles it before setting it down on the edge of a platform. **CANDIDE** falls on his knees next to the handkerchief.)*

Oh spite…what dreadful dole is here?

CACAMBO. A piece of cloth.

CANDIDE. Her mantle, what? stained with blood.

CACAMBO. Midsummer, Act 5, scene 3?

CANDIDE. No. Lady Cunegonde's handkerchief. She dropped this handkerchief for me once. I swoon.

(He swoons.)

CACAMBO. Lean on me, sir.

*(**CACAMBO** helps **CANDIDE** back to the platform and sets him down next to the severed head.)*

CANDIDE. Dead. Ah, where is the best of worlds now?

(The head begins to talk. Yes, there is a convenient trap door in the platform, and as **CACAMBO** *stands in front to block the view, and* **CANDIDE** *wails over the handkerchief to distract the audience, the prop head is exchanged for a real one.)*

BULGARIAN SOLDIER 1. It's just war. War is an unavoidable thing in the best of worlds.

CANDIDE. Who said that?

CACAMBO. Who said what?

BULGARIAN SOLDIER 1. Private misfortunes are public benefits; so that the more individuals suffer, the greater the general good. It's God's way. If I may speak as a detached observer?

CANDIDE. By all means.

BULGARIAN SOLDIER 1. A country is destroyed, another becomes richer. A castle is ransacked, some soldiers have extra coin to spend.

CANDIDE. That's enough!

BULGARIAN SOLDIER 1. Sorry. You look confused. Go ahead. Ask me anything. I'm quite a visionary now. Ahead of my time.

CANDIDE. Will mankind always massacre one another this way?

BULGARIAN SOLDIER 1. Will hawks always eat pigeons?

CANDIDE. There is a great difference between pigeons and men.

BULGARIAN SOLDIER 1. Not at all. Baron Thunder-ten-Tronckh's ancestors stole his castle at bayonet point. Now we've taken it back. That's war.

CANDIDE. Well, we should abolished that.

BULGARIAN SOLDIER 1. Abolish war? What about us Bulgarians? All we know is war. Do you want to put us all out of work?

CANDIDE. I don't care. I want to see my Cunegonde again.

BULGARIAN SOLDIER 1. It's all about you, is it? Well, I've suffered, too.

(**CANDIDE** *walks away.*)

But should we change policy because I die or you die or some woman is ravished and ravished and ravished and...

(**CANDIDE** *rushes back and strangles the head.*)

CANDIDE. Stop. God never gave mankind twenty-four pounders, nor bayonets.....

(**CACAMBO** *pulls* **CANDIDE** *away from the head.*)

CACAMBO. Master.... Give it up...

(**CANDIDE** *crumples to the floor to try and collect himself. An old beggar,* **DR PANGLOSS**, *enters. His nose is eaten away and replaced with a tin replica. His clothes are worn and ragged.*)

PANGLOSS. Can you lend a hand? To a fellow down on his luck?

(**CACAMBO** *picks up a severed hand from the carnage and hands it to* **PANGLOSS**.)

CACAMBO. Here you go.

PANGLOSS. No.

CACAMBO. An arm and a leg. That's about the best we can do.

PANGLOSS. A bit of money, perhaps....

(*He stops as he recognizes* **CACAMBO** *then* **CANDIDE**.)

Do you not recognize me?

CANDIDE. Um....

PANGLOSS. I am Doctor Pangloss, your old teacher.

CANDIDE. Doctor Pangloss? But look at you? Your nose.

PANGLOSS. Gone.

CANDIDE. (*embracing* **PANGLOSS**) How horrible war is.

PANGLOSS. Oh, it wasn't the war.

CANDIDE. No?

PANGLOSS. It was love.

CANDIDE. But how could love produce so hideous an effect?

PANGLOSS. A fast acting, highly contagious, disease…

CANDIDE. Pardon?

PANGLOSS. Syphilis.

CANDIDE. *(quickly taking a slide-step away)* Oh, my.

PANGLOSS. You remember Pacquette? In her arms I tasted Paradise, which produced this Hell.

> *(PAQUETTE comes out on stage and waves.)*

She was infected with an ailment from a learned Franciscan,

> *(A MONK comes out , lines up next to PAQUETTE, and waves to the audience.)*

Who derived it from an old countess,

> *(THE MADAME comes out in turn and waves.)*

Who had it of a captain,

> *(THE PIRATE SKIPPER comes out and waves.)*

The pirate from an Amazon,

> *(THE AMAZON QUEEN comes out and waves.)*

Who had it in a direct line from Christopher Columbus, himself;

> *(COLUMBUS comes out and waves.)*

COLUMBUS. Bonjourno.

PANGLOSS. Who had it from…

> *(A SHEEP comes out and waves.)*

Well enough of this line…

> *(The lineup exits.)*

CANDIDE. Surely this is not a necessary ingredient of the best of all possible worlds.

PANGLOSS. I beg to differ. It was a thing unavoidable, for if Columbus had not caught, while discovering America, this disease, and brought it back to Europe, we should not have chocolate, which was also brought back with him. And chocolate is undeniably a part of the best of all possible worlds.

Scene Four

(A slide on the scrim: A picture of a ship going off the edge of the world accompanied by the words, "Chapter Four: How Candide Met James the Anabaptist.")

JAMES THE ANABAPTIST. Chapter Four:

(The dead bodies get up, dust themselves off, and exit, clearing debris from the stage as they go.)

How Candide Met James the Anabaptist…After a series of Picaresque adventures too complicated to describe…

PANGLOSS. Who are you?

JAMES THE ANABAPTIST. I'm the new narrator.

PANGLOSS. What happened to the old ones?

JAMES THE ANABAPTIST. Yourself being riddled with disease, and the Baron and Baroness, who narrated a bit, having been violently killed during the war, Paquette enslaved, and the Old Woman left for dead, I thought you'd need a new narrator.

PANGLOSS. A bit cheeky.

JAMES THE ANABAPTIST. I'm James the Anabaptist.

*(Stagehands bring in a two part, cartoonish, cardboard boat to surround **JAMES THE ANABAPTIST**, **CANDIDE**, **PANGLOSS** and **CACAMBO**.)*

CANDIDE. Where are we now?

JAMES THE ANABAPTIST. We are on a boat bound for Portugal.

PANGLOSS. How did we get there?

JAMES THE ANABAPTIST. As I pointed out, it's much too complicated.

CANDIDE. I see.

JAMES THE ANABAPTIST. And to tell you the truth, my story doesn't involve war or dismemberment or romances, only acts of charity. And who wants to see that? Surely not these people.

(He introduces himself to the audience.)

I'm James the Anabaptist.

PANGLOSS. *(losing patience)* We know.

CACAMBO. What's an Anabaptist?

PANGLOSS. Don't encourage him.

JAMES THE ANABAPTIST. A member of a radical movement of the 16th-century Reformation that viewed baptism, not as a religious communion, but solely as an external witness to a believer's conscious profession of faith.

PANGLOSS. A bit obscure, don't you think?

JAMES THE ANABAPTIST. *(to* CANDIDE*)* Suffice it to say, I saved your life.

CANDIDE. Oh, thank you.

JAMES THE ANABAPTIST. *(to* PANGLOSS*)* And I paid for the bleedings and enemas to contain your disease of love.

CACAMBO. He *is* looking a bit better.

JAMES THE ANABAPTIST. And what do you suppose is my reward for all this good work?

PANGLOSS. We have no idea.

JAMES THE ANABAPTIST. Well, I'll narrate it for you. Suddenly, the winds blew; the sails were blown into shreds, and the masts cracked. The vessel was a total wreck.

(The cardboard boat breaks in half. CANDIDE, PANGLOSS *and* CACAMBO *cling safely to the bow.* JAMES *falls overboard.)*

By a sudden jerk of the ship, James the Anabaptist was swept overboard.

PANGLOSS. Thank God.

JAMES THE ANABAPTIST. You can still save me.

CANDIDE. I'll save you –

PANGLOSS. But Candide was prevented by the philosopher Pangloss, who said; "This tempest has been made with exact purpose that James the Anabaptist and would-be narrator could be drowned."

*(*JAMES THE ANABAPTIST *floats away, noisily drowning.* TOWNSPEOPLE *enter. The boat is carried off.)*

PANGLOSS. Here we are in Portugal.

CANDIDE. Why are we here?

CACAMBO. We don't know. Pangloss killed off the narrator before he could tell us.

Scene Five

(Slide: A picture of the Lisbon Earthquake of 1755, accompanied by the words, "Chapter Five: An Eart-quake, and How Candide Underwent Public Flagellation." **PAQUETTE** *and* **OLD WOMAN** *enter.)*

PAQUETTE. Chapter Five: An Eartquake, and how Candide underwent public flagellation.

CANDIDE. What?

CACAMBO. She said, "An earthquake."

CANDIDE. Not that part. The part about public flagellation.

(The earth shakes. During the earthquake, large chunks of Styrofoam rock fly onto the stage. **TOWNSPEOPLE** *are hit and killed, littering the stage. Dead bodies are everywhere.)*

OLD WOMAN. The earth trembled under their feet.

PAQUETTE. And as the townspeople ran out of their houses, large sheets of flame and cinders from the volcano covered the streets.

CANDIDE. Let's help them.

(The **NARRATORS** *exit.* **CANDIDE** *and* **CACAMBO** *pull bodies out of the rubble.* **PANGLOSS** *comforts one* **MAN** *trapped under a block. The* **MAN** *dies as* **PANGLOSS** *speaks to him. The* **INSPECTOR GENERAL** *and the two* **EXECUTIONERS** *enter and witness the exchange.)*

PANGLOSS. Let me comfort you, sir. If there is a volcano at Lisbon, it could be in no other spot; all this is for the very best, and it is impossible...

(The **MAN** *dies loudly. Is there any other way?)*

Well, it's for the best.

INSPECTOR GENERAL. If everything is best, there is no such thing as original sin and the fall of man.

PANGLOSS. The fall of man is part of the system of the best of worlds.

INSPECTOR GENERAL. That is as much as to say, sir, you do not believe in free will.

(The menacing **EXECUTIONERS** *sandwich* **PANGLOSS.***)*

PANGLOSS. Free will is consistent with the system; for it was necessary we should be free, for –

(The **EXECUTIONERS** *knock out* **PANGLOSS** *with a bonk to the head.)*

CANDIDE. What are you doing?

(The **EXECUTIONERS** *bonk* **CANDIDE** *on the head. The* **INSPECTOR GENERAL** *leads them off, dragging* **CANDIDE** *and* **PANGLOSS** *behind.* **CACAMBO** *follows at a safe distance. The* **GRAND INQUISITOR** *enters with the* **VICEROY**. *He talks to the dead bodies.)*

GRAND INQUISITOR. Thank you. Oh, no this is too much. Rise. Rise.

VICEROY. Your majesty, I do not think they are bowing.

GRAND INQUISITOR. Bowing, genuflecting, what's in a word.

VICEROY. They are the victims of the volcano.

GRAND INQUISITOR. Oh, of course. I will comfort them.

VICEROY. I don't think…

GRAND INQUISITOR. My fellow Portuguese, we come among you to give hope to the surviving –

VICEROY. Your majesty, these subjects appear to have died in this morning's event.

GRAND INQUISITOR. How rude. Did no one tell them I was coming?

VICEROY. Sir, half of Lisbon is in ruins.

GRAND INQUISITOR. I see.

VICEROY. We must find a way to assure that there are no more earthquakes.

GRAND INQUISITOR. Pass a decree. There will be no more earthquakes under penalty of death. Etc., etc.

INSPECTOR GENERAL. *(entering)* It will not be that easy.

VICEROY. Inspector…your specialness.

INSPECTOR GENERAL. I am merely the servant of the law. God's Law. These recent disturbances in the earth are a clear sign that God is unhappy .

GRAND INQUISITOR. How do you suggest we appease your Inspectorship? I mean, God.

INSPECTOR GENERAL. Auto-da-fe.

GRAND INQUISITOR. What's that?

VICEROY. Everyone in 18th century Portugal knows what an Auto-da-fe is.

GRAND INQUISITOR. Let's pretend for a moment I'm not from 18th century Portugal. Let's pretend I'm from, say, _____ *(the name of your town and state).*

INSPECTOR GENERAL. Auto-da-fe: Burning a few people alive by a slow fire, and with great ceremony. It's an infallible preventive for earthquakes.

VICEROY. Burning people alive? Prevents earthquakes?

INSPECTOR GENERAL. Three fires, at most, should do the trick.

GRAND INQUISITOR. I like it.

(suddenly serious)

Oh…will *we* be among those burned?

INSPECTOR GENERAL. If we wanted to prevent ignorance, we'd burn you. But we want to prevent earthquakes.

GRAND INQUISITOR. On with the Auto-da-fe.

*(The square fills with people getting ready for the Auto-da-fe. Even the dead bodies get up and join the celebration. A stake for burning is rolled out. The **EXECUTIONERS** lead in the **BISCAYAN**.)*

INSPECTOR GENERAL. Ladies and Gentlemen, our first contestant at the bar. A Biscayan who married his own godmother.

VICEROY. How do you plead?

BISCAYAN. I couldn't help myself. She was still young and hot. She's right over there.

GODMOTHER. Hello, Grand Inquisitor.

GRAND INQUISITOR. She is very young.

BISCAYAN. And very hot.

GRAND INQUISITOR. Not as hot as you'll be. Death by fire.
And all your worldly goods, chattel, wives, etc. are for-
feit to me.... I mean, to the church.

EXECUTIONER 2. You have been found guilty of marrying a
hot mama.

EXECUTIONER 1. Prepare to have your sins purged with fire.

EXECUTIONER 2. Do you have anything to say?

BISCAYAN. I die a free man, secure in my love.

(The **EXECUTIONERS** *tie him to the stake.)*

And my wife will stand here beside me in the flames
and die rather than live on alone...

(Everyone looks over at his wife. She is flirting with the
GRAND INQUISITOR.*)*

Pumpkin?

GODMOTHER. Well, as you say, I am still very young... and
hot.

BISCAYAN. What?

GODMOTHER. I will occasionally miss you though.

GRAND INQUISITOR. And could we have some music? I like
music.

(Drums roll and Bagpipes begin.)

BISCAYAN. But...awwwwww.

(The **EXECUTIONERS** *light the fire. They slowly raise a
piece of cloth painted like fire up over the* **BISCAYAN**'s
*head. When they drop the cloth back down, only a
charred skeleton remains. Everyone cheers.)*

GRAND INQUISITOR. Next.

INSPECTOR GENERAL. A wealthy merchant who picked the
bacon out of his stew before eating.

VICEROY. How do you plead?

MERCHANT. I don't like bacon. So sue me.

GRAND INQUISITOR. Death by fire. All your wealth etc, etc.

MERCHANT. Wait. Wait. Normally I like bacon, but that morning it looked a little off. A little green around –

EXECUTIONER 2. *(tying the* **MERCHANT** *to the stake)* That's what they all say.

MERCHANT. Don't I even get a last meal? Bacon, that's what I want. If I could just have one more slice of bacon. Ummm. Yummy, yummy!

EXECUTIONER 1. Hold still.

(Bagpipes begin. The fire starts to rise. The **MERCHANT** *tries to blow it out. He is burned alive, screaming. The flames recede to reveal a charred skeleton. Everyone cheers.)*

GRAND INQUISITOR. I like this Auto-da-fe. Next.

INSPECTOR GENERAL. We have two contestants competing for our final spot. An old man who is here for speaking his mind, and a young man for seeming to approve of what he said.

(They bring out **CANDIDE** *and* **PANGLOSS**.*)*

GRAND INQUISITOR. Which one has a bigger estate.

INSPECTOR GENERAL. Both are paupers.

GRAND INQUISITOR. Hot wives?

INSPECTOR GENERAL. Neither married. But speaking one's mind is a severe crime even for a pauper.

GRAND INQUISITOR. Then kill the old one, and can we at least flog the young one.

(The **EXECUTIONERS** *pull the* **INSPECTOR GENERAL** *aside.)*

EXECUTIONER 2. Sir, we have a slight problem.

INSPECTOR GENERAL. What is it?

EXECUTIONER 1. We ran out of fire wood.

INSPECTOR GENERAL. Get some more.

EXECUTIONER 2. It rained last night,

EXECUTIONER 1. All the wood is wet.

EXECUTIONER 2. We weren't expecting to use so much fuel with the man who wouldn't eat bacon.

INSPECTOR GENERAL. Imbeciles.

EXECUTIONER 2. Thank you.

EXECUTIONER 1. Now, we *can* shoot him.

EXECUTIONER 2. Or we can hang him.

EXECUTIONER 1. But I don't think we can burn him.

INSPECTOR GENERAL. Very well, hang him.

(EXECUTIONER 2 raises his hand and waits to be called upon.)

Yes?

EXECUTIONER 2. We don't have a rope.

INSPECTOR GENERAL. Use the rope you were going to tie him to the stake with?

EXECUTIONER 1. Ah! I guess that's why you're the Inspector General, and we're just the executioners.

EXECUTIONER 2. *(announcing to crowd)* Ladies and gentlemen. There has been a change in plans. The old man will not be burned at the stake, he will be hung by the neck until dead.

EXECUTIONER 1. But, as a special added feature, we will flog the young man who listened to him.

EXECUTIONER 2. Also, while we are very adept at burning, we have no experience at hanging prisoners.

EXECUTIONER 1. So it's likely to be a very, very slow and painful death.

(The crowd murmurs with approval.)

INSPECTOR GENERAL. Enough. Begin the ceremony.

(Bagpipes begin. One **EXECUTIONER** *ties* **CANDIDE** *to the stake for flogging. The other takes* **PANGLOSS** *to a high platform where a rope is looped around his neck. Being inexperienced at hanging, and only having a short rope, the* **EXECUTIONER** *makes* **PANGLOSS** *hold the end of his own rope.* **PANGLOSS** *raises his arm high in the air until the rope is taught. He twists slowly, choking.* **PAQUETTE,** *the* **OLD WOMAN,** *and* **CUNEGONDE** *step forward, out of the crowd. They wear veils.)*

PAQUETTE. Candide was flogged to the tune of bagpipes, and Pangloss was hanged, which is not a common custom at these solemnities.

(CUNEGONDE can't bear to watch CANDIDE flogged and rushes off.)

OLD WOMAN. Just then, there was an aftershock, which made most dreadful havoc.

(The earth shakes. People exit screaming. CANDIDE is left with the hanged body of PANGLOSS. CACAMBO helps CANDIDE off the stake. PANGLOSS falls to the platform, dead.)

CACAMBO. If this is the best of all possible worlds, what are the others?

(The veiled OLD WOMAN and PAQUETTE help CACAMBO support the groggy CANDIDE.)

OLD WOMAN. *(to CANDIDE)* Take courage, child, and follow me.

PAQUETTE. We will take you to safety.

OLD WOMAN. They walked him to a lonely mansion surrounded with moats and gardens.

PAQUETTE. Up the back stairs, into a small, but richly furnished apartment.

(They lead CANDIDE to CUNEGONDE. She also has a veil over her face.)

OLD WOMAN. Remove the veil...

(CANDIDE tries to remove the OLD WOMAN's veil.)

Not my veil, idiot...Hers.

(She points to CUNEGONDE. CANDIDE removes her veil and is overcome with joy.)

PAQUETTE. At first they could only express themselves with sighs, tears, and exclamations.

(CANDIDE and CUNEGONDE make joyous noises but form no words.)

Scene Six

(Slide: A country house with the words, "Chapter Six: What happened to Cunegonde.")

OLD WOMAN. Chapter Six: What happened to Cunegonde.

(They leave **CANDIDE** *and* **CUNEGONDE** *alone.)*

CANDIDE. Thank God, you are alive, and you have not been ravished!

CUNEGONDE. Well, I'm alive.

CANDIDE. I thought they ripped open your body?

CUNEGONDE. Like a gutted pig. But this does not always prove mortal.

CANDIDE. But…

CUNEGONDE. Shh. I will tell you all…In flashback.

(Pleasant, flashback music begins. **FLASHBACK CUNE-GONDE** *ballet dances onto the stage. She wears a sign around her neck that reads, "Flashback Cunegonde." She pantomimes as* **CUNEGONDE** *describes.)*

CANDIDE. Who is that?

CUNEGONDE. That is flashback Cunegonde. Isn't she pretty.

CANDIDE. Not so pretty as real life Cunegonde.

CUNEGONDE. Shh. Suddenly, Bulgarians attack.

(The music changes. The **BULGARIAN ARMY** *rushes in. Opposite are the* **FLASHBACK HEINRICH**, **FLASHBACK BARON** *wearing signs.)*

CANDIDE. I thought Westphalia attacked first.

CUNEGONDE. First, second, what's the difference? My father and brother were cut to pieces trying to save me.

*(***FLASHBACK BARON** *and* **FLASHBACK HEINRICH** *run away. The* **BULGARIANS** *repeatedly ravish* **FLASHBACK CUNEGONDE** *in slow motion.)*

I cried, I struggled, I scratched, I would have torn the tall, handsome Bulgarian's eyes out, not knowing that what happened to me was a customary thing in war.

One brutal soldier, enraged at my resistance, gave me
a wound in my left thigh with his sword, the mark of
which I still carry.

CANDIDE. Methinks I long to see it.

CUNEGONDE. You shall, but let me proceed.

CANDIDE. Pray do.

(*A Bulgarian* CAPTAIN *takes* FLASHBACK CUNE-
GONDE. *The* ARMY *exits.*)

CUNEGONDE. A Bulgarian captain took me as a prisoner of
war to his quarters. I...I washed his linen,

(CUNEGONDE*'s voice quivers as she recalls doing chores.*
FLASHBACK CUNEGONDE *pretends to wash clothes. She
uses her charm to get the* CAPTAIN *to do her work for her.*)

CANDIDE. No!

CUNEGONDE. And cooked his food,

(FLASHBACK CUNEGONDE *pretends to cook. She burns
her finger. The* CAPTAIN *kisses the booboo, then takes
over cooking for her.*)

CANDIDE. My poor innocent.

CUNEGONDE. And scrubbed his floors.

(FLASHBACK CUNEGONDE *starts to scrub. She breaks
a nail. The* CAPTAIN *jumps in to do her work for her.*)

CANDIDE. No!

CUNEGONDE. Yes.

(FLASHBACK CUNEGONDE *points out a spot that the*
CAPTAIN *has missed.*)

He grew tired of me and sold me to a rich Banker,
named Don Issachar.

(FLASHBACK DON ISSACHAR, *wearing a sign, enters
proudly. He gives cash to the* CAPTAIN, *who exits
happily. He then gives a gift of jewels to* FLASHBACK
CUNEGONDE.)

Don Issachar, the Banker, showed me great kindness in
hopes of gaining my favors; but he couldn't prevail on
me to yield so easily.

CANDIDE. My virtuous Cunegonde.

CUNEGONDE. Of course he was very, very persistent;

(**FLASHBACK DON ISSACHAR** *lavishes necklaces of jewels on* **FLASHBACK CUNEGONDE.**)

CANDIDE. What?

CUNEGONDE. And he did arrange for me to be reunited with my servants.

(**FLASHBACK OLD WOMAN** *and* **FLASHBACK PAQUETTE,** *wearing signs, step in and wave.*)

CANDIDE. What?

CUNEGONDE. Neither can I deny that he was handsome, and had a soft, white skin…Oh, but he was very stupid, and knew nothing of philosophy.

CANDIDE. Thank goodness.

CUNEGONDE. Enter the Grand Inquisitor.

(**FLASHBACK GRAND INQUISITOR,** *with sign, enters.*)

CANDIDE. Hey, he's the one responsible for Dr. Pangloss's death and my flogging….

(**CANDIDE** *suddenly realizes* **CUNEGONDE** *may have been ravished by him, too.*)

No!

CUNEGONDE. Yes. His lordship threatened Don Issachar with an Auto-da-fe; in short, my Banker was frightened into a compromise, and they agreed that I would belong to both of them in common.

(*The flashback characters shake hands in agreement and all exit.*)

CANDIDE. Like a time share?

CUNEGONDE. Even so. The Banker would have me Monday, Wednesday and Saturday. The Grand Inquisitor the rest of the week, although Tuesdays I like some time to myself, and it is unclear whether the space from Saturday Night to Sunday Morning belongs to the Banker or the Inquisitor.

CANDIDE. What does it matter, as long as, hitherto, you have withstood them both.

CUNEGONDE. *(hedging)* Oh, I have...mostly.

(She brightens.)

Each and every time they asked me to marry them, I said,... "No!"

CANDIDE. And what if *I* asked you to marry me?

CUNEGONDE. If you asked me, Candide, I would most certainly say –

(DON ISSACHAR enters carrying a gift.)

Uh oh...

CANDIDE. What a strange response.

CUNEGONDE. I mean, "Uh oh." It's Don Issachar.

CANDIDE. The Banker? He's rather taller and handsomer than his flashback counterpart.

CUNEGONDE. And richer.

DON ISSACHAR. My dearest Cunegonde. I have a little bauble for...

(He stops when he sees CANDIDE.)

Who is this? Speak, thou Galilean Slut!

CUNEGONDE. *(introducing the two)* Candide, Don Issachar. Don Issachar, Candide.

DON ISSACHAR. *(suddenly friendly)* Glad to meet you.

CANDIDE. Heard so much about you.

DON ISSACHAR. Likewise.

(DON ISSACHAR suddenly slaps CANDIDE.)

Let your "hands stray" with my woman!

CUNEGONDE. Let's be civil.

ISSACHAR. The Grand Inquisitor was not enough for thee?

CUNEGONDE. *(taking the present from DON ISSACHAR)* Ooh. For me? What is it?

DON ISSACHAR. *(suddenly sweet)* A trinket. Diamonds. You seemed so grateful last time.

CANDIDE. She's not your woman.

DON ISSACHAR. *(suddenly angry)* What can this *boy* offer you?

CANDIDE. I offer her nothing. Nothing but love.

*(**CUNEGONDE** sits on the floor and opens the present, not watching the two men.)*

DON ISSACHAR. Then you will die…for love….

(He draws his sword.)

CANDIDE. I warn you, I am no novice.

*(Having no weapon, **CANDIDE** takes off his shoe and threatens **DON ISSACHAR**.)*

Ha! I have been one day at war. I strangled a severed head. I also ran the Bulgarian Gauntlet in a scene deleted for time.

DON ISSACHAR. And I have killed twenty-seven men in duals such as these.

CANDIDE. Twenty-seven? You sure?

DON ISSACHAR. It's not the sort of thing you forget.

CANDIDE. I must admit, you have me at a disadvantage in that regard.

DON ISSACHAR. How many have you killed?

CANDIDE. In round numbers?

DON ISSACHAR. Yes.

CANDIDE. Well, there is only one round number, isn't there?

DON ISSACHAR. Let me correct myself: soon to be twenty-eight men killed.

*(**CUNEGONDE** opens the jewels and lets out a squeal of delight. **DON ISSACHAR**, startled by the noise, drops his sword.)*

CUNEGONDE. Ahh! Thank you!

DON ISSACHAR. *(to **CUNEGONDE**, suddenly sweet)* Do you really like it?

CANDIDE. Excuse me. We're busy here. You dropped your sword….

(**CANDIDE** *picks up* **DON ISSACHAR**'s *sword and holds it out for him.*)

DON ISSACHAR. Thanks.

(**DON ISSACHAR** *turns back to* **CANDIDE**. *As he does he takes a step forward and impales himself on his own outstretched sword.*)

CANDIDE. Oops.

DON ISSACHAR. Ahhh! Love…to die for…Love.

(*He dies.* **PAQUETTE, CACAMBO** *and* **OLD WOMAN** *return to find a dead body on the floor.*)

OLD WOMAN. Holy Virgin!

GRAND INQUISITOR. (*offstage*) Oh, Cunegonde. Yoo hoo?

CACAMBO. Who is that?

PAQUETTE. The Grand Inquisitor.

OLD WOMAN. Is it past midnight already?

GRAND INQUISITOR. (*offstage*) My jewel. My darling.

(*He enters wearing a ballet tutu and bearing a gift.*)

It's Sunday morning. Are you ready for…I…

(*He stops short when he sees* **CANDIDE**.)

CUNEGONDE. Candide, Grand Inquisitor, Grand Inquisitor…

GRAND INQUISITOR. We've met.

CUNEGONDE. (*taking the gift, excitedly*) For me?

(*She sits down to open the package.*)

GRAND INQUISITOR. (*never taking his focus off* **CANDIDE**) Is that a dead body at your feet?

OLD WOMAN. Had not Pangloss been hanged, he would have given Candide most excellent advice in this emergency; for he was a profound philosopher.

PAQUETTE. But, since he is not here, a sudden thought came into Candide's head.

CANDIDE. (*spoken very, very quickly*) If this holy man should call assistance, I shall most undoubtedly be consigned to the flames, and Miss Cunegonde may perhaps meet with no better treatment: besides, he was the cause of my being so cruelly whipped; he is my rival; and as I have now begun to dip my hands in blood, I will kill away.

OLD WOMAN. This whole train of reasoning was clear and instantaneous; so that, without giving time to the Inquisitor to recover from his surprise, Candide ran him through the body.

*(**CANDIDE** stabs the **GRAND INQUISITOR** without looking.)*

CANDIDE. Oops.

CUNEGONDE. This is a fine piece of work. What were you thinking?

CANDIDE. *(pointing at the audience)* They heard. It seemed reasonable at the time.

CACAMBO. We must hurry and get away.

OLD WOMAN. There are horses in the stable.

CACAMBO. I will hitch them to the wagon.

OLD WOMAN. Madame Cunegonde, do not forget your box of jewels. We will need all your wealth for our journey. Though I have lost one buttock, we will ride tonight, to Cadiz.

CACAMBO. What's in Cadiz?

OLD WOMAN. A ship to take us to the new world.

*(They hurry out, leaving **CANDIDE** standing alone over the dead bodies.)*

CANDIDE. Maybe we should leave a note, or something.

*(They rush back in and pull **CANDIDE** off with them. The dead bodies rise and exit.)*

Scene Seven

(Slide: A picture of a sea port accompanied by the words, "Chapter Seven: Meanwhile." PANGLOSS enters, the noose still around his neck.)

PANGLOSS. Chapter Seven. A chapter simply known as "Meanwhile." Because we keep saying, "Meanwhile."

(The EXECUTIONERS enter and watch PANGLOSS narrate.)

Meanwhile, just past midnight, the executioners meet in secret at the University of Coimbra. The medical lab.

EXECUTIONER 1. You're supposed to be dead.

PANGLOSS. Sorry.

(PANGLOSS dies. The EXECUTIONERS pick him up and carry him over to the SURGEON, who enters opposite.)

EXECUTIONER 2. Here it is.

SURGEON. Lay it down on the operating table. I'll just get my scalpels.

(They plop PANGLOSS onto a table.)

It's missing the nose.

EXECUTIONER 1. Ninety percent of its interesting parts are still intact.

SURGEON. It's riddled with disease.

EXECUTIONER 2. All the better for studying disease, I'd say.

SURGEON. You promised me a healthy corpse.

EXECUTIONER 2. I see how it is. We risk everything.

EXECUTIONER 1. Look like fools with the whole wet wood thing. "Oh, we're out of wood." Like we don't know our job.

SURGEON. Fine. What is he? A pickpocket? A murderer?

EXECUTIONER 1. He was put to death for being a philosopher.

SURGEON. No, no, no! No Philosophers. You cut into them, there's a lot of hot air that comes out. It's the devil in them, I wager.

EXECUTIONER 1. Did I say philosopher? I meant pig thief.

SURGEON. You can't fool me. What else you got?

EXECUTIONER 2. Just him.

(They place the charred remains of a burned body on the table.)

SURGEON. That's all?

EXECUTIONER 1. It was a slow week.

SURGEON. All right.

(The **SURGEON** *weighs which corpse to buy. It's a very close decision)*

I'll take...the philosopher.

EXECUTIONER 1. If you don't mind my asking, what are you going to do with it?

SURGEON. I'm going to dissect it.

EXECUTIONER 2. Mind if we watch?

SURGEON. If you wish.

EXECUTIONER 1. Cool.

SURGEON. I start with an incision from his navel to his clavicle.

(The **SURGEON** *takes a large butcher knife and cuts into* **PANGLOSS**' *chest. Blood spurts out.)*

Strange, it shouldn't spurt that much.

(The two **EXECUTIONERS** *faint at the sight.)*

Oh lord. Get up. Get up, you....

*(***PANGLOSS** *rises from the dead.)*

It's the devil. Ahhhhh!

(The **SURGEON** *runs out.* **PANGLOSS** *staggers off, the butcher knife still impaled in his chest.* **PAQUETTE** *enters.)*

PAQUETTE. Meanwhile, on the road to Cadiz, Candide hit a bump in the road.

(CANDIDE, CUNEGONDE, CACAMBO, *and the* **OLD WOMAN** *enter in a wagon being pulled by two* **HORSES**.

A **LUCKY NUN** *enters opposite. She moonwalks past the wagon to give the effect of motion. The wagon hits a bump in the road. The scene enters slow motion.* **CUNE-GONDE***'s jewelry box bounces off the back of the wagon and flies through the air. A* **STAGEHAND**, *dressed head to toe in black, picks up the jewelry box, makes it sail into the air and bounce to a stop on the stage floor. Then back to fast motion.)*

CANDIDE. What was that?

PAQUETTE. A bump in the road.

CANDIDE. I thought so.

PAQUETTE. Unbeknownst to our travelers, Cunegonde's box of jewels bounced high in the air and landed at the feet of a passing Nun.

(The **LUCKY NUN** *finds the jewel box at her feet and opens it.)*

A pious woman, she had taken vows of poverty and silence, she did what any nun in a similar position would do.

LUCKY NUN. Wee ha! Mama Mia! Thank you Lord, thank....

(A **BEGGAR** *enters opposite. The* **LUCKY NUN** *stifles her joy and hides the jewels behind her.)*

BEGGAR. Alms for the poor. Alms...

(The **LUCKY NUN** *motions like she has made a vow of silence.)*

PAQUETTE. She's taken a vow of silence.

BEGGAR. Of course, good Sister.

(The **LUCKY NUN** *offers the* **BEGGAR** *a crust of bread from her bag)*

Thank you. The lord will reward your kindness.

(The **BEGGAR** *exits.)*

Alms for the poor...

LUCKY NUN. Weeeee Haw!

(She dances off.)

PAQUETTE. Meanwhile…Back at Cunegonde's mansion.

(The dead bodies of **DON ISSACHAR** *and the* **GRAND INQUISITOR** *walk on and fall down dead in their old spots. The* **INSPECTOR GENERAL** *and* **VICEROY** *enter and look over the corpses.)*

INSPECTOR GENERAL. Whoever it was, meant to disgrace the Grand Inquisitor by dressing him in women's clothes and placing him next to a dead…Banker.

VICEROY. Actually, the Grand Inquisitor loved to dress in… You are absolutely correct. They went out of their way to disgrace him.

INSPECTOR GENERAL. I will make a vow, here and now. We will not eat. We will not sleep. We will not give in to the joys of the mortal world, until we have found these killers and brought them to justice.

VICEROY. We?

INSPECTOR GENERAL. You and I.

VICEROY. I thought, actually, I'd hang around Lisbon, maybe get a job in the entertainment…

INSPECTOR GENERAL. No! We will be inseparable on our quest.

VICEROY. All right, but, these, "joys of the mortal world?" What do they include, exactly?

INSPECTOR GENERAL. Come, our destiny awaits us.

(They exit. The **DEAD BODIES** *get up, dust off and exit.)*

PAQUETTE. Meanwhile, Candide and Cunegonde, arrive at the port of Cadiz.

*(***CANDIDE, CUNEGONDE, CACAMBO,** *and* **HORSES** *enter.)*

Once there, they discovered the treasure box was missing.

ALL. No…

OLD WOMAN. *(entering opposite)* Oh, pipe down. I have come from the dock and I have bad news, I have worse news, and I have good news.

PAQUETTE. Good news can wait.

OLD WOMAN. Right, bad news first. There are no ships to take us to the New World.

PAQUETTE. No ships? What are all those in the harbor?

OLD WOMAN. Reserved for military transport. It seems the Franciscan Friars in Paraguay have formed an army and are in revolt. An equal army must be sent to put them down. So we are stuck here without a penny, without shelter, without a bite of food.

CUNEGONDE. Gee, what could be worse than that?

OLD WOMAN. The Inspector General, as we speak is on his way to arrest us.

CACAMBO. How do you know.

OLD WOMAN. I watched the last scene from the side curtain.

CANDIDE. And the good news?

OLD WOMAN. I know a really good recipe for horse stew!

(*The* **HORSES** *freak out.*)

CANDIDE. Wait. There must be a better way.

(*A* **DRILL SERGEANT** *marches a group of out-of-step* **WOMEN SOLDIERS** *onto the stage.*)

DRILL SERGEANT. That is awful. Stay together. How do you expect to beat my little sister if you can't even walk in rhythm? Step it up, ladies.

(*One* **SOLDIER** *breaks down in tears.*)

What? Are you crying? Oh, that'll scare 'em. Oh, can't you just hear the Franciscan Friars running for shelter. "Oh, help, help! Somebody's crying at us."

CANDIDE. Excuse me, sir.

DRILL SERGEANT. Can't you see I'm berating my troops?

CANDIDE. It will only take a second.

DRILL SERGEANT. Very well.

(*to his troops*)

At ease. Pretend to smoke if you have them.

(*The* **WOMEN SOLDIERS** *rest and pantomime smoking.*)

CANDIDE. My name is…Captain Candide. And this is my company.

DRILL SERGEANT. As in company for a tea party?

CANDIDE. No.

DRILL SERGEANT. As in company for a sleep over.

CANDIDE. Sir, as in "army company."

DRILL SERGEANT. Don't make me laugh. I thought we were scraping the bottom of the barrel with these recruits, but you? You are no more an army than flying pigs are birds!

CANDIDE. We know the Bulgarian Drill…

DRILL SERGEANT. The Drill? You know…The Drill? You?

CANDIDE. I guess we'll just offer our services to the Franciscan Friars.

DRILL SERGEANT. Don't make me laugh.

CANDIDE. Drill with me!

(**CANDIDE** *leads his entourage in the Bulgarian Drill. Even the* **HORSES** *drill along. The* **DRILL SEARGEANT** *falls to his knees.*)

DRILL SERGEANT. My Captain, I apologize. Command me, and I will obey.

CANDIDE. We will need immediate passage to South America.

DRILL SERGEANT. There is a ship leaving right away.

CANDIDE. Right away is not soon enough for the Bulgarian Company.

DRILL SERGEANT. As you wish.

(*All exit except the* **OLD WOMAN** *who walks centerstage and stands staring down the audience for a dramatic moment. Finally she speaks.*)

OLD WOMAN. Meanwhile.

(*She exits. The* **EXECUTIONERS** *drag on the* **LUCKY NUN** *and hold her up for the* **INSPECTOR GENERAL** *and* **VICEROY**)

INSPECTOR GENERAL. Torture her until she talks.

VICEROY. She has taken a vow of silence, your Inspectorship.

INSPECTOR GENERAL. So she says.

VICEROY. She, actually, didn't say it, since that would break her vow of –

INSPECTOR GENERAL. Silence.

VICEROY. Yes, that was the vow. A vow of –

INSPECTOR GENERAL. I mean, you! Silence. Torture her. Make her hold her hands palm up and strike down upon them with a ruler, saying, "Little Giorgio, pay attention in class..." Not that that would give me any pleasure.

VICEROY. We don't have a ruler.

INSPECTOR GENERAL. What do you have?

VICEROY. We have a meter stick.

INSPECTOR GENERAL. Hit her with the meter stick.

(*The* **EXECUTIONERS** *raise meter sticks threateningly.*)

LUCKY NUN. Wait! The box fell off a coach bound for Cadiz. Five people. Two horses. Four sheep. They called the man Candide. One of them appeared to be missing a buttock. Not that I'm an expert.

INSPECTOR GENERAL. Lies! You will regret that you did not cooperate.

LUCKY NUN. I'm telling the truth.

VICEROY. She may be. They could hire a ship in Cadiz to take them to America.

LUCKY NUN. Please, I'll tell you anything.

INSPECTOR GENERAL. Oh, will you?

LUCKY NUN. Anything.

INSPECTOR GENERAL. What is the circumference of a circle divided by the diameter approximated to five places?

LUCKY NUN. I don't know that.

INSPECTOR GENERAL. Flog her.

(*They flog her until the next scene begins.*)

Scene Eight

*(Slide: a picture of ancient sea monsters and a boat at sea accompanied by the words, "Chapter Eight: On a Ship in the Atlantic, Bound for the Coast of South America." **PANGLOSS** enters. The noose is still around his neck. The butcher knife is still impaled in his chest. The **EXECUTIONERS** continue to pummel the **LUCKY NUN** in the background.)*

PANGLOSS. *(to **EXECUTIONERS**)* That's enough.

(The others exit.)

Chapter eight: On a ship in the Atlantic, bound for the coast of South America.

*(He exits. **CUNEGONDE, CANDIDE, CACAMBO, PAQUETTE,** the **DRILL SERGEANT,** and the **OLD WOMAN** take their places in order on the ship. The **HORSES** form a second row behind them. The ship is a four by eight foot raised platform. The actors are squished together like sardines, with no room to move.)*

CANDIDE. All will be well. Soon we will be married.

CUNEGONDE. But I have met with such terrible treatment that I have almost lost all hopes of a better life.

OLD WOMAN. What murmuring and complaining.

CUNEGONDE. Excuse me?

*(**CUNEGONDE** sidles her way down the length of the boat, bumping each traveler along the way, like a good actress, always keeping herself facing front and down stage, until she is next to the **OLD WOMAN**.)*

Surely I have suffered more than any other woman. Excuse me.

*(She sidles back to **CANDIDE**.)*

OLD WOMAN. You suffer?

*(The **OLD WOMAN** sidles over to **CUNEGONDE**, her one buttock big enough to knock the other travelers off their balance.)*

OLD WOMAN. *(cont.)* If you had suffered half what I have, you might have some complaint.

(CUNEGONDE drives the OLD WOMAN back to the other side of the ship, both bumping those behind them.)

CUNEGONDE. Unless you had been ravished by two hundred Bulgarians, had received two deep wounds in your belly, had lost two fathers, and two mothers, and to sum up all, had two lovers whipped at an Auto-da-fe, I cannot see how you could be more unfortunate than I.

(CUNEGONDE sidles back to CANDIDE's side.)

OLD WOMAN. Well let me tell you.

PAQUETTE. Oh, no, here it comes.

OLD WOMAN. I have more good news.

(The OLD WOMAN sidles to the center of the ship.)

Since we are trapped on this boat crossing the Atlantic, we have ample time to hear...The Story of The Old Woman with No Name and Only One Buttock.

(FLASHBACK OLD WOMAN enters to act everything out.)

CANDIDE. Who's that?

OLD WOMAN. *(not paying attention to the flashback actor)* Me.

CANDIDE. No. Who's that?

(He points at FLASHBACK OLD WOMAN.)

OLD WOMAN. It's Flashback Old Woman with No Name and Only One Buttock. Now I begin. You would not believe me would you, if I told you I was the daughter of Pope Urban the Tenth?

PAQUETTE. You can say that again.

OLD WOMAN. I was the daughter of Pope Urban the Tenth.

PAQUETTE. I meant the part about believing you.

OLD WOMAN. My mother was the Princess of Palestrina. I was brought up in a castle, compared with which the castle of the German Baron would not be fit for stables.

(FLASHBACK OLD WOMAN is not meeting OLD WOMAN's standards. The OLD WOMAN climbs down from the ship and takes the sign from around FLASHBACK OLD WOMAN's neck. She puts it around her own neck.)

OLD WOMAN. *(cont.)* I will self-flashback, now.

(FLASHBACK OLD WOMAN exits.)

At 14, I already began to inspire men with love. My breast began to take its right form, and such a breast! White, firm, and formed like that of the Venus de' Milo!

PAQUETTE. Out of solid marble?

OLD WOMAN. My maids, when they dressed me, used to faint into an ecstasy in viewing me from behind; and all the men longed to be in their places...

(PAQUETTE sneaks down from the ship and goes to speak directly to the audience as the OLD WOMAN drones on in the background.)

PAQUETTE. This is quite a long story. Trust me. She tells it whenever anyone will let her. While we're waiting for her to finish, we're going to try out something new, We call it, "Special Feature, Deleted Scenes." She won't even know we're gone.

OLD WOMAN. *(in background)* I was contracted in marriage to a sovereign prince of Massa Carrara. Such a prince! as handsome as myself, sweet-tempered, agreeable, witty, and in love with me over head and ears. I loved him, too, as our sex generally do for the first time, with rapture, transport, and idolatry....

(PAQUETTE sneaks out in front of the curtain and motions for the crew to close it behind her. She holds her finger up to her lips to indicate the audience needs to be quiet. The curtain is closed.)

PAQUETTE. As we told you, *Candide* is a Picaresque novella and there's no possible way to adapt every scene to the stage. But, we can offer you *one* deleted scene from *Candide* as a "Special Feature." Can I get the farm animals out here. They agreed to help me. Anything to get a few extra lines, you know. It works like this. We'll list deleted scenes and you vote on which one you want to see.

(The **SHEEP** *enter, holding signs with the scene titles. They read the signs aloud to the audience.)*

SHEEP 1. Scene One: James the Anabaptist performs acts of charity, and they talk a lot.

PAQUETTE. You remember James from Chapter four.

SHEEP 2. Scene Two: Candide pays a visit to Seignor Pococurante, a Noble pessimist and they talk a lot.

PAQUETTE. Pococuante has some real stinging commentary about John Milton, the author of *Paradise Lost.*

SHEEP 3. Scene Three: Candide has supper with six former heads of state, and they talk a lot.

PAQUETTE. It's like having Millard Fillmore, Neville Chamberlain, Disraeli, Kaiser Wilhelm, Mussolini, and Charles de Gaulle sitting around talking politics. And our last choice.

SHEEP 4. Scene Four: Naked girls are chased by monkeys.

PAQUETTE. Which is about, well, naked girls being chased by monkeys. Don't blame me, Voltaire thought it up. All right. Let's vote. Only cheer for one....

*(***PAQUETTE*** stands behind each ***SHEEP*** encouraging the audience to vote.)*

Who would like to see Scene One? Scene Two? Scene Three? Scene Four?

(The cheers are overwhelmingly for the monkey scene. The **SHEEP** *leave, looking back accusingly at* **PAQUETTE***.)*

Wow. We really didn't expect that outcome, so we don't have anything prepared. We're not saying there's anything wrong with your choice. We just didn't expect it.

(A **SHEEP** *comes out and whispers something to Paquette.)*

Well, tell James the Anabaptist that the audience didn't want to see it.

(The **SHEEP** *whispers something else.* **PAQUETTE** *nods.)*

PAQUETTE. *(cont.)* All right. They're throwing something together in the back...They need a few minutes. Let me check on the Old Woman.

(She motions for the curtain to open. The **OLD WOMAN** *still rambles on. She swings in a seat created by the arms of two handsome men.)*

OLD WOMAN. ...I was enchanting; I was beauty itself, and back then I had my virginity. This precious flower, Upon our arrival at Morocco we found that kingdom deluged with blood....

PAQUETTE. Just as I thought.

(She motions for the curtain to close on the **OLD WOMAN**.*)*

So why don't you just take a little break. Get some refreshments at the snack bar. I won't tell her you've gone. When the sheep are ready, we'll flash the lights, or something to let you know. I'd say, we got a good fifteen minutes.

*(***PAQUETTE*** sneaks back in through a crack in the curtain. We get a glimpse of the* **OLD WOMAN** *still yammering.)*

OLD WOMAN. I had not been long a slave when the plague, which had made the tour of Africa, Asia, and Europe, broke out at Algiers with redoubled fury...

Intermission

ACT II

Prologue

*(The curtains open on the same sign and the **OLD WOMAN** mid-action. The other seafarers stand with stunned looks of boredom on their faces. The **OLD WOMAN** acts out a flashback scene with the **EUNUCH**.)*

OLD WOMAN. I crawled over a heap of corpses, and lay down overwhelmed with horror, and quite naked. Suddenly a figure of a man was towering over me. A soldier, who sighed and muttered these words...

EUNUCH. What a time to be a Eunuch!

*(**PAQUETTE** sneaks back to the audience as the **OLD WOMAN** continues. The curtain closes behind her.)*

PAQUETTE. As you can see, this is proceeding slowly. I think she's about 60% finished. While she continues, we have that deleted scene prepared. It's a little rough, but, we'll see. The full name of the chapter is: What Happened to Our Two Travelers with Two Girls, Two Monkeys, and the Savages, Called Oreillons.

*(Two **SHEEP** enter with pink ribbons in their hair. the other two **SHEEP** follow wearing monkey masks.)*

These are the girls and the monkeys. All right girls. Get naked.

*(The two **SHEEP** take the pink ribbons out of their hair, the total extent of their attempt to get naked. **PAQUETTE** admonishes those in the audience who wanted more.)*

Oh, get a life.

*(**CANDIDE** and **CACAMBO** sneak around the curtain.)*

CANDIDE. Are you ready for us?

CACAMBO. Thanks, Paquette.

PAQUETTE. Places.

> (*The* **SHEEP** *exit and* **CANDIDE** *and* **CACAMBO** *overact walking through the jungle.*)

Candide and his valet had already passed the frontiers, far off the beaten path. Suddenly they heard voices.

> (*The naked* **SHEEP** *enter, skipping.*)

GIRLS. Ohh, aaagh! Oh, we are running.

PAQUETTE. The cries proceeded from two young women who were tripping, disrobed, along the mead.

> (*The two* **MONKEYS** *enter in pursuit.*)

While two monkeys followed close at their heels biting at their limbs.

> (*The* **MONKEYS** *cut off the* **GIRLS**, *accompanied by much screaming and monkey sounds.*)

Candide was touched with compassion. Accordingly, he took up his double-barreled Spanish gun, pulled the trigger, and laid the two monkeys on the ground.

> (**CANDIDE** *shoots. The* **MONKEYS** *stagger. The* **GIRLS** *freeze is shock. The* **MONKEYS** *speak, mortally wounded, sinking to the floor and fading with each word.*)

MONKEY 1. He shot me?

MONKEY 2. I can't believe he shot me.

MONKEY 1. Humans!

MONKEY 2. Well, you can't blame a whole species for the actions of one. That would be like blaming us for all those monkeys jumping on a bed.

MONKEY 1. Call for a doctor

MONKEY 2. And the doctor said…No more monkeys… jumping on the bed.

> (*The* **MONKEYS** *expire.*)

CANDIDE. God be praised, my dear Cacambo, if I have committed a sin in killing an Inquisitor and a Banker, I have made ample amends by saving the lives of these two distressed damsels.

CACAMBO. Did you notice something funny about those monkeys?

CANDIDE. Like what?

CACAMBO. Nothing. Except they were talking.

CANDIDE. Now that you mention it.

CACAMBO. Look!

(*The* **GIRLS** *fall to their knees and cry over the fallen* **MONKEYS**.)

GIRL 1. You….You killed them.

GIRL 2. You killed our boyfriends.

CANDIDE. Your boyfriends? Well, that's surprising.

CACAMBO. Master, you are surprised at everything.

PAQUETTE. Suddenly, they saw themselves surrounded by fifty naked, hungry cannibals, called Oreillons, armed with bows and arrows.

(*The two* **HORSES** *enter, waving weapons and giving war yelps.*)

Where are the rest of the Oreillons?

HORSE 1. We ran out of farm animals.

PAQUETTE. They were surrounded by two, very angry, very hungry Oreillons.

HORSE 1. Let's kabob them with some baby carrots and some of those little pink potatoes.

HORSE 2. I say boil them like lobster with a nice, tangy butter sauce.

(*The* **HORSES** *continue to argue about the proper way to cook the humans. The* **GIRLS** *join in.* **CANDIDE** *and* **CACAMBO** *talk over their chatter.*)

CANDIDE. Ah! What would Pangloss say? Everything is for the best; but I must confess it is something hard to be away from Miss Cunegonde, and to be spitted like a rabbit.

CACAMBO. Pangloss might, in fact, say, "Run!"

CANDIDE. Good call, Cacambo.

(CANDIDE and CACAMBO run off. The farm animals suddenly notice they are alone.)

HORSE 2. That was unlucky.

HORSE 1. I was hungry, too. Could eat a hors – Well, you know.

(They look down at the dead MONKEYS.)

GIRL 1. Alright, Monkey stew it is.

(The farm animals exit, dragging the dead MONKEYS with them.)

PAQUETTE. That's the end of our feature. I hope you liked it. Of course, if it was a really good scene, it wouldn't have been deleted in the first place. But it did have violence and nudity, so it wasn't a total loss. Let's check and see what they're up to back stage.

(The curtain opens on the OLD WOMAN in the midst of still talking. She acts out the scene with the three CANNIBAL SOLDIERS.)

OLD WOMAN. Thus being reduced to extreme famine, they found themselves obliged to eat their own belts, then their shoes, rather than violate their oath, never to surrender. But soon they were hungry again.

(The CANNIBAL SOLDIERS bonk the OLD WOMAN on the head. She falls with her knees and face on the floor and her buttock straight up in the air. CANNIBAL 2 raises a knife to the OLD WOMAN.)

CANNIBAL 1. All right. We got thigh, we got drumstick. We got breast meat.

(All the CANNIBAL SOLDIERS shudder at the OLD WOMAN's breasts.)

CANNIBAL 3. What about that.

(He points at the buttock.)

CANNIBAL 2. That's the buttock.

CANNIBAL 3. I'm quite fond of rump roast.

(All the **CANNIBAL SOLDIERS** *grunt with approval.)*

CANNIBAL 1. Rump roast it is.

(He saws into the **OLD WOMAN***'s buttock.)*

OLD WOMAN. The soldiers had scarcely started the meal, when the Russians attacked and I was rescued by –

PAQUETTE. And that is why she only has one buttock. Give it up, ladies and gentlemen.

OLD WOMAN. But there's so much more.

PAQUETTE. Oh, look. We're here. South America.

Scene One

(Slide: A picture of an old South American sea port accompanied by the words, "Chapter Nine: How Candide Was Obliged to Leave the Fair Cunegonde in Buenos Aires.")

PAQUETTE. Chapter Nine: How Candide was obliged to leave the fair Cunegonde in Buenos Aires.

(All exit. DON FERNANDO, the original Ladies Man, enters with a SEXY WOMAN on each arm.)

SEXY WOMAN 1. Enter Don Fernando d'Ibaraa y Figueora y Mascarenes y Lampourdos y Souza.

SEXY WOMAN 2. The great Dictator, I mean, the Governor of the Portuguese Colonies.

DON FERNANDO. This is surely the best of all possible worlds...for me.

(The SEXY WOMEN laugh.)

Let me tell you how it works. I see an apple?

SEXY WOMEN. He takes an apple.

DON FERNANDO. I see a horse?

SEXY WOMEN. He takes a horse.

DON FERNANDO. I see a hard working indigenous people, living in freedom long before the American Revolution?

(There is a long pause while the SEXY WOMEN think.)

I enslave them.

SEXY WOMEN. He enslaves them.

DON FERNANDO. I see a woman?

SEXY WOMEN. He takes a woman.

DON FERNANDO. But the women? They don't seem to mind.

(Behind his back, the SEXY WOMEN indicate they mind. A MESSENGER enters.)

MESSENGER. Your Excellency.

DON FERNANDO. *(taking out a pistol and threatening the* **MESSENGER***)* Messenger, you have ten seconds to impress me before I shoot you, just because I can.

MESSENGER. Sir, the natives are revolting.

DON FERNANDO. I know that, though I would call them more...disgusting. Four seconds. Three, two...

MESSENGER. Sir, they have taken up arms and joined the rebellion.

DON FERNANDO. With the Franciscan Friars?

MESSENGER. Yes. They say you're ignoring them and their complaints.

DON FERNANDO. Ignoring them? Why, I whip them every day.

MESSENGER. That may be what they're complaining about.

DON FERNANDO. Surely the Franciscan Friars whip their slaves, too.

MESSENGER. They haven't got any.

DON FERNANDO. Whips?

MESSENGER. Slaves.

DON FERNANDO. No slaves?

MESSENGER. Men are free.

DON FERNANDO. But not the women?

MESSENGER. The women, too.

DON FERNANDO. I knew they were trouble from the moment those Franciscan Friars arrived. All this, "Let's open a school and teach them how to read."

SEXY WOMAN 1. Filling their heads with ideas.

SEXY WOMAN 2. Educating the masses?

DON FERNANDO. I ask you, did we torture and ravish, pillage and plunder, just to give the land back?

SEXY WOMEN. No.

DON FERNANDO. *(to* **MESSENGER***)* All right. Take this message back to the Natives. If they cooperate, I'll only whip them every other day, except on Sundays when I'll whip them twice.

MESSENGER. Yes, sir.

(**DON FERNANDO** *shoots the* **MESSENGER** *in the buttock.*)

DON FERNANDO. I did that to prove I was a man of action.

(**CANDIDE, CACAMBO, CUNEGONDE, PAQUETTE,** *the* **OLD WOMAN** *and the* **DRILL SERGEANT** *enter with the* **HORSES.**)

SERGEANT. Your Excellency. We're here from Portugal with the reinforcements.

DON FERNANDO. Thank God. Where's the army.

SERGEANT. This *is* the army. And this is Captain Candide.

(**DON FERNANDO** *sees* **CUNEGONDE** *and is instantly taken. He brushes past* **CANDIDE** *and kisses* **CUNE-GONDE***'s hand.*)

DON FERNANDO. My name is Don Fernando d'Ibaraa y Figueora y Mascarenes y Lampourdos y Souza y Chalupa

CUNEGONDE. Oh, my.

DON FERNANDO. Captain Candide, your wife is surely the most beautiful woman in the world.

CANDIDE. Oh, she's not my wife.

DON FERNANDO. How very honest, Captain. If she were *not* my wife, I would lie and say she was, just to keep her away from the clutches of other, much, much sexier men.

CANDIDE. Miss Cunegonde is my fiancée. Perhaps Your Excellency will preside over the ceremony.

DON FERNANDO. I intend, more than you imagine, to preside over Miss Cunegonde.

(**CACAMBO** *steps in and pulls* **CUNEGONDE** *away from* **DON FERNANDO.**)

CACAMBO. If you'll excuse us. We need to get our accommodations in order.

OLD WOMAN. (*flirting with* **DON FERNANDO**) I have one buttock.

(**DON FERNANDO** *scoots away from her. The entourage exits.*)

DON FERNANDO. I must have her.

MESSENGER. The old woman?

DON FERNANDO. Not the old woman. Cunegonde.

MESSENGER. She's engaged.

DON FERNANDO. Why is it, what cannot be easily attained is always more desirable?

MESSENGER. Everything is easily obtained by you.

DON FERNANDO. Go to Captain Candide. Tell him he must immediately go into the field and inspect the troops. Send Miss Cunegonde to me.

MESSENGER. Oh, I see. He'll be away and…

(They laugh. **MESSENGER** *limps off.* **DON FERNANDO** *talks directly to the audience.)*

DON FERNANDO. What? I sense you do not like me. But I did not kill this Candide, and I could have. I know what you're thinking. I only didn't kill him because he may be more use to me alive…You're right.

*(***CUNEGONDE** *enters.)*

CUNEGONDE. You desire to see me?

DON FERNANDO. Ah, but I desire so much more.

CUNEGONDE. Sir, I am engaged to Candide.

DON FERNANDO. And yet he does not marry you. Was there no Priest in Cadiz? Was there no captain aboard the ship to do the ceremony?

CUNEGONDE. It *is* peculiar that he's made no attempt to fulfill our promises.

DON FERNANDO. *I* would not hesitate. I am ready to give you my hand in marriage, or "otherwise"; whatever is more agreeable to a young lady of your prodigious beauty.

CUNEGONDE. Oh, dear.

DON FERNANDO. Shhh. Do not answer right away. I'll give you a half an hour. Your answer will not only seal your fortunes, but those of Candide.

CUNEGONDE. How so?

DON FERNANDO. In half an hour I will decide whether to send Captain Candide into the jungle to face the fierce Franciscan Friars and certain death, or station him here, in Buenos Aires.

(**CUNEGONDE** *exits, pursued by* **DON FERNANDO.**)

PAQUETTE. Cunegonde immediately returned to her servants and made them aware of the Governor's offer. While she was thus occupied, a small boat entered the harbor.

(*The* **INSPECTOR GENERAL** *and* **VICEROY** *enter in a cartoonish, cardboard rowboat. Townspeople enter to meet the boat. The* **VICEROY** *rows the boat and the* **INSPECTOR GENERAL** *stands in the bow like George Washington. The* **VICEROY** *is very tired, having just rowed across the Atlantic.*)

INSPECTOR GENERAL. Townspeople of Buenos Aires. I have some questions.

SEXY WOMAN 1. We don't like questions.

SEXY WOMAN 2. We came here, to South America to escape questions.

SEXY WOMAN 1. Who are you to ask us questions?

INSPECTOR GENERAL. Good question. I am the Inspector General of the Portuguese Inquisition.

(*The townspeople run away screaming in fear.*)

VICEROY. Maybe we should rest and start again in the morning.

INSPECTOR GENERAL. Rest? I laugh at rest. Do you know when we will rest?

VICEROY. My guess is, we will never rest.

INSPECTOR GENERAL. Oh, we *will* rest. When we string this killer up by his cuticles and slap the bottom of his feet as a warning to other runaways.

VICEROY. Then we'll rest?

INSPECTOR GENERAL. Not then. Not until we see him tied to the stake and cleansed by fire.

VICEROY. Then we'll rest?

INSPECTOR GENERAL. And after the fire we will hang him from the gallows and watch his charred body twist in the wind.

VICEROY. Then…

INSPECTOR GENERAL. And when we bring the body down, we will chop off his lifeless head.

VICEROY. Then…

INSPECTOR GENERAL. And we will fill his body with candies and little treats and trinkets, and hang him from a rafter, and give the local children heavy sticks to hit him like a piñata!

VICEROY. And then?

INSPECTOR GENERAL. And then what?

VICEROY. I thought there was more.

INSPECTOR GENERAL. There's no more. We are civilized people. So after we place his head on a spike above the castle moat and watch the crows pluck out his eyes…we *will* rest.

*(**DON FERNANDO** enters with the **MESSENGER**.)*

DON FERNANDO. Welcome, sir. Word has spread of your arrival. I am Don Fernando d'Ibaraa y Figueora y Mascarenes y Lampourdos y Souza, y Casadilla de Salsa Verde, Governor of Buenos Ares.

INSPECTOR GENERAL. We are looking for a group of murderers. We have this evidence.

*(**VICEROY** holds up the jewel box.)*

VICEROY. We took it from a Nun on the road to Cadiz.

INSPECTOR GENERAL. Unfortunately she died a painful death before she could tell us the meaning of the strange inscription on the box.

VICEROY. It says "Miss Cunegonde's big box of jewels."

DON FERNANDO. Now empty, I see. Gentlemen, no one fitting that description has landed in our port. But I will certainly keep an eye out.

(to MESSENGER*)*

DON FERNANDO. *(cont.)* Prepare a room for our guests to rest and serve his Excellency some dinner.

INSPECTOR GENERAL. We will not rest until justice has been served.

DON FERNANDO. Just ice? Well, your choice. Serve them Just ice for dinner.

MESSENGER. That was a shockingly bad pun, sir.

DON FERNANDO. I see a joke, I take a joke.

*(*THE MESSENGER *leads them away.* DON FERNANDO *shoots the* MESSENGER *in the other buttock, just because he can.* CANDIDE *enters with* CACAMBO.*)*

Captain! Thank goodness!

CANDIDE. You know, I went to the field, but there weren't any troops.

DON FERNANDO. Never mind. The Inspector General is here. Run away immediately, or you will die.

CANDIDE. I won't go without Cunagunde.

DON FERNANDO. Sometimes, to protect the ones we love, we must leave the ones we love behind. The jungle is a treacherous place for a woman. She will be safe here. As Governor, I will not allow her to be ill-treated by anyone else; therefore leave her in my capable hands.

CANDIDE. You promise to look after her?

DON FERNANDO. As if she were my own fiancée. Someone comes. Run!

*(*CANDIDE *and* CACAMBO *run out through the audience.* CUNEGONDE *enters.)*

CUNEGONDE. Is that Candide running away into the jungle?

DON FERNANDO. Where?

CUNEGONDE. Out there…

(She points at the audience members.)

Among the natives.

DON FERNANDO. So it is. What motivated him to leave you?

CUNEGONDE. I can think of no reason.

DON FERNANDO. You've hit on it. He has left you for no
    reason. But take comfort, I am still here.

(They exit. He stops to talk to the audience.)

I see a woman. I take a woman.

(He laughs and follows CUNEGONDE *off.)*

Scene Two

(Slide: a picture of South American natives accompanied by the words, "Chapter Ten: Among the Jesuit Revolutionaries." The **OLD WOMAN** *and* **PAQUETTE** *enter.)*

OLD WOMAN. Chapter Ten: Among the Jesuit Revolutionaries.

*(***CANDIDE** *and* **CACAMBO** *enter running.)*

PAQUETTE. Candide and Cacambo ran deep into the jungle, to a place that few civilized men had seen.

*(***REVOLUTIONARIES** *jump out from behind the platforms, guns drawn. They dress like modern gang-bangers rather than 18th century natives.)*

A place beyond the rule of Portugal.

REVOLUTIONARY 1. Throw down your weapons, or we will kill you.

CACAMBO. May I ask, how will you proceed if we *do* throw down our weapons?

REVOLUTIONARY 1. Kill you, anyway. But first we like to watch you tremble.

CANDIDE. Stand back! I know the Bulgarian Drill. Drill with me, Cacambo.

(They do "The Drill.")

CACAMBO. I don't think it's working.

REVOLUTIONARY 2. What is this?

CANDIDE. I warn you. We can do it faster.

(They do it faster.)

REVOLUTIONARY 2. This is the jungle, Holmes.

REVOLUTIONARY 1. Fancy stepping does not scare us here.

REVOLUTIONARY 2. We serve the Rebel Jesuit of Paraguay. We are revolutionaries.

ALL REVOLUTIONARIES. Viva la Revolution.

REVOLUTIONARY 2. We have our own drills here.

(A **REVOLUTIONARY** *beat-boxes and they all break into dance.* **CACAMBO** *pulls* **CANDIDE** *aside.)*

CACAMBO. They speak of the very man you were sent to fight.

CANDIDE. You sure?

CACAMBO. The Rebel Jesuit of Paraguay. The leader of the Franciscan Friars. You were going to fight against him; now let's turn and fight for him.

*(*CACAMBO *interrupts the* **REVOLUTIONARIES***.)*

Excuse me.

REVOLUTIONARY 2. You dare come between a Revolutionary and his celebration?

CACAMBO. Sirs, we're here, not as your enemy, but to serve the Rebel Jesuit of Paraguay.

REVOLUTIONARY 1. How?

CANDIDE. Advise him on the art of the Bulgarian Drill.

REVOLUTIONARY 2. Do you know what the Rebel Jesuit of Paraguay does to Bulgarians?

CANDIDE. No.

REVOLUTIONARY 2. He strips their skin off one layer at a time and laughs while they scream in pain.

CACAMBO. It's a good thing we're not Bulgarians, then.

REVOLUTIONARY 1. But he's nice to the Bulgarians. The Portuguese? He pulls their eyeballs out with pliers, then sends small cockroaches in through the open sockets to nest in their brains.

CACAMBO. We are neither Bulgarian or Portuguese.

REVOLUTIONARY 2. English?

CANDIDE. No.

REVOLUTIONARY 1. Spaniard?

CACAMBO. No.

REVOLUTIONARY 2. French?

CANDIDE. No.

REVOLUTIONARY 1. What are you?

CANDIDE. German.

REVOLUTIONARY 1. A moment please.

(*He pulls his comrade aside.*)

What is the usual procedure with Germans?

REVOLUTIONARY 2. I don't know. Germans are so peace-loving.

(**HEINRICH** *enters wearing a monk robe and hood.*)

HEINRICH. I'll tell you what we do with Germans.

ALL REVOLUTIONARIES. Rebel Jesuit of Paraguay!

(*They all fall on the ground and grovel.*)

HEINRICH. We invite Germans in for bratwurst and chee.... ee...eeze

(*He recognizes* **CANDIDE** *and gives him a bear hug.*)

CANDIDE. If you must ravish me, do it quickly.

HEINRICH. Don't you recognize me? Westphalia. The Castle Thunder-ten-tronckh.

CANDIDE. Strange. *I* was born at the Castle Thunder-ten-tronckh.

HEINRICH. It's me, Heinrich.

CANDIDE. Oh, heavens!

HEINRICH. (*to* **REVOLUTIONARIES**) This is my brother from another mother!

(**REVOLUTIONARIES** *jump up and shoot their guns in the air.*)

Leave us, comrades, so I may talk to my brother.

(*The* **REVOLUTIONARIES** *exit whooping.*)

CANDIDE. But how did you escape death?

(**HEINRICH** *steps out, very dramatically.*)

HEINRICH. Never shall I forget that horrible day. That day on which I saw my father and mother barbarously....

CACAMBO. Excuse me.

HEINRICH. Yes?

CACAMBO. Is this going to be a very long flashback.

(**CACAMBO** *motions to the audience.*)

They've already had intermission.

HEINRICH. I can make it faster.

CANDIDE. Please.

HEINRICH. *(quickly)* My body was taken to a chapel. A Jesuit sprinkled me with holy water, which was very salty. A few drops went into my eyes, and up I sat. The Priest died of a heart attack. I filled the vacancy.

CACAMBO. That was short.

HEINRICH. Thank you.

CANDIDE. But how did you get here to Paraguay.

HEINRICH. Following the Jesuits. You know, I was very handsome; and I dare say all the Reverend Fathers took a great fancy to me.

CACAMBO. You mean…like.

HEINRICH. Oh, yes, they were very kind.

CACAMBO. Oh?

HEINRICH. Oh, yes. Always checking to see that my bandages were changed and clean. Waking me up in the middle of the night to make sure the bed was soft enough. Making sure the bath water was…

CANDIDE. Whoa!…Hey, I almost forgot. Your sister, Cunegonde?

HEINRICH. Yes. Her belly slit open.

CANDIDE. She's alive.

HEINRICH. Where?

CANDIDE. With the Governor of Buenos Aires.

HEINRICH. Oh, ecstasy. Someday, we will enter that city, sword in hand, and rescue my sister, Cunegonde!

CANDIDE. Ah! That would be perfect, for then we could be married.

HEINRICH. And kill the…What? Why would I want to marry you?

CANDIDE. Not me. Cunegonde.

HEINRICH. Why would I marry my sister?

CANDIDE. No, I will marry Cunegonde.

HEINRICH. You!

(HEINRICH becomes suddenly violent.)

You have the impudence to marry my sister? My sister, who can trace back her family tree seventy-two generations!

(He draws his sword and pursues CANDIDE.)

How dare you!

CANDIDE. Be civil, Brother.

HEINRICH. You dare call me brother?

CANDIDE. I was hoping it might have a calming affect.

HEINRICH. You were wrong!

(HEINRICH lunges at CANDIDE. The sword twists and HEINRICH stabs himself. He dies. The REVOLUTION-ARIES are heard offstage.)

REVOLUTIONARY 1. *(off)* Is anything wrong?

CACAMBO. Quick, hide him.

(CANDIDE drapes the dead brother over his shoulder. CACAMBO stands behind the corpse and pretends to talk for him and moving HEINRICH's mouth and arms, like a puppet. The REVOLUTIONARIES enter with guns drawn.)

REVOLUTIONARY 2. We heard some shouting.

CACAMBO. *(as HEINRICH.)* Nothing wrong here.

REVOLUTIONARY 1. Is that you, Comrade?

REVOLUTIONARY 2. You sound different.

CACAMBO. *(using a deep voice like HEINRICH)* Just choked up with happiness to see my long lost brother from another mother.

(CANDIDE hugs the body. The REVOLUTIONARIES suddenly realize CANDIDE and HEINRICH might have a thing going.)

REVOLUTIONARY 1. Pardon, your excellency. We had no idea you two were...were...

REVOLUTIONARY 2. We are not ones to make judgements. Excuse us.

(They exit. **CANDIDE** *and* **CACAMBO** *drop the body and run.)*

CACAMBO. Run!

Scene Three

(Slide: A picture of a city of gold accompanied by the words, "Chapter Eleven: El Dorado." The dead body gets up and leaves. The OLD WOMAN *and* PAQUETTE *enter.* CANDIDE *and* CACAMBO *run in slow motion during the narration.)*

OLD WOMAN. Chapter Eleven: El Dorado.

PAQUETTE. And so they ran even deeper into the jungle, past monkeys chasing naked women and cannibals threatening to boil them alive.

OLD WOMAN. At last, they came to a little river, the Amazon.

PAQUETTE. They tried to cross, but the current was swift.

OLD WOMAN. Down they swept, into raging rapids.

PAQUETTE. Over towering waterfalls.

OLD WOMAN. Through underground tunnels.

PAQUETTE. Before the river opened up again and was calm.

OLD WOMAN. They climbed ashore only to find themselves on a spacious plain, bounded by inaccessible mountains.

CACAMBO. Inaccessible mountains?

OLD WOMAN. That's what I said.

*(CACAMBO *and* CANDIDE *collapse on the ground.)*

CACAMBO. Then, by definition, we shall never leave this valley.

CANDIDE. Cunegonde!

*(CANDIDE *pounds on the ground. He becomes obsessed with handful of dirt.)*

Cacambo! Do you see what I see?

*(AMAZON PRINCESSES *run by playing with a golden ball.* CACAMBO *notices them, but* CANDIDE *is still looking at the dirt.)*

CACAMBO. I'm not even sure I see what I see.

CANDIDE. No, Cacambo! Do you see what I see?

(He forces **CACAMBO** *to look at the dirt.)*

CACAMBO. A handful...of gold!

(They scream for joy. They look around there is gold eveywhere. **PAQUETTE** *and* **OLD WOMAN** *empty bags of crumpled up, brightly colored paper across the stage.)*

Look! The rocks! Unless I mistake, this is a precious Ruby! This an emerald! A diamond!

CANDIDE. I am rich, Cacambo!

PAQUETTE. Indeed, they had stumbled into a valley where the soil was pure gold, where the rocks were all jewels.

OLD WOMAN. Riches so precious that no theater company could afford to duplicate the effect.

PAQUETTE. And therefore the gold dust had to be pantomimed.

OLD WOMAN. And the jewels were represented by ordinary wads of colored paper.

*(***PAQUETTE** *and* **OLD WOMAN** *exit.* **CANDIDE** *falls on the ground and makes dirt angels in the gold.* **CACAMBO** *stuffs wads of paper jewels into his shirt. The* **AMAZON PRINCESSES** *playing ball come back.)*

CACAMBO. Look out! Natives. Hide the treasure.

(They stuff more jewels into their clothes creating a fat and lumpy look. **CANDIDE** *addresses the girls.)*

CANDIDE. Hello, oh lovely native girls.

(The girls look at **CANDIDE** *as if he is strange.)*

They don't seem to understand.

CACAMBO. Let me try.

*(***CACAMBO** *approaches the girls and bows. He speaks to them very slowly, like they are space aliens.)*

We hungry and tired. Bring food. We pay you well. We very, very wealthy men, with huge jewels.

*(***CACAMBO** *offers the girls some wadded up paper. The girls scream and run away.)*

PAQUETTE. When the native princesses got back home, they told their mother, the Queen of El Dorado, about the strangers.

(The QUEEN *enters with the* SHEEP. *The* SHEEP *wear pink ribbons in their hair. The* PRINCESSES *rush up to her and point opposite where* CANDIDE *and* CACAMBO *stuff their shirts with jewels.)*

PRINCESS 2. They talked very, very slowly.

PRINCESS 1. As if they had never lived among civilized people.

PRINCESS 2. They had strange growths all over their torso. Tumors.

PRINCESS 1. Then they offered us common rocks in exchange for food.

QUEEN. Odd. Are you sure.

PRINCESS 2. Yes. I fear they are touched.

PRINCESS 1. Here they come now.

(The QUEEN *and* PRINCESSES *hide as* CANDIDE *and* CACAMBO *move center.)*

CACAMBO. Master, look at this city.

CANDIDE. Every house a Palace.

CACAMBO. The cobblestones.

CANDIDE. Gold.

CACAMBO. The bricks...

QUEEN. Good afternoon.

(She startles them. They drop their arm loads of jewels.)

CANDIDE. We didn't do it.

CACAMBO. We found them, honest.

QUEEN. *(to her daughters)* Alas, I fear it is worse than you have told me.

*(*CANDIDE *and* CACAMBO *throw themselves on the ground.)*

CACAMBO. Please, don't hurt us.

QUEEN. Gentlemen, rise. We will not harm you.

(They offer the jewels back to her.)

No...keep them.

CACAMBO. What?

QUEEN. Take as many as you like.

*(**CACAMBO** goes crazy and starts grabbing all the jewels he can, stuffing them in his shirt.)*

CANDIDE. You must be a very wealthy Queen.

QUEEN. Everyone is equal here. We are all kings and queens in El Dorado.

CANDIDE. All kings and queens. Well, that's good, too. Who are the priests?

QUEEN. We are all priests.

CANDIDE. No, you don't understand, who's the person who burns you alive if you don't believe what he does.

QUEEN. We all believe the same, here in El Dorado.

CANDIDE. But who builds the mansions?

QUEEN. We all build. Each contributes according to their talent.

CANDIDE. Have you no working class, no servants?

QUEEN. We are all servants.

CANDIDE. I don't like that as well as the king/queen thing.

QUEEN. No person is above any other, here.

CANDIDE. How strange. Well, we are very hungry. But we can pay.

*(He offers her jewels. All laugh at his offer, even the **SHEEP**.)*

QUEEN. Come with me. We'll find a meal to suit you.

*(They exit as **PAQUETTE** enters.)*

PAQUETTE. Back in Buenos Aires, Don Fernando was about to take a woman.

*(**PAQUETTE** exits. **DON FERNANDO** chases **CUNE-GONDE** onto the stage. They play cat and mouse a bit before she is cornered.)*

CUNEGONDE. You will never take me…

(**DON FERNANDO** *dangles a large jewel before her.*)

Oooohh!

(*She admires the gem but is suddenly sad.*)

Oh.

DON FERNANDO. What is it?

CUNEGONDE. It clashes with my necklace.

DON FERNANDO. You haven't got a necklace.

CUNEGONDE. Not yet.

(*She struts away, pouting.* **DON FERNANDO** *starts to follow her. The* **INSPECTOR GENERAL** *pops up with the* **VICEROY**. *They carry flashlights and shine them in* **DON FERNANDO** *'s eyes.*)

INSPECTOR GENERAL. Amazing, Governor, how some things are always just out of our reach.

DON FERNANDO. What are you doing out this late at night?

VICEROY. We never rest. Never…Never.

INSPECTOR GENERAL. You'll be happy to know, despite your interference, we're heading into the jungle to pursue Captain Candide, for we acquired information that he went this direction.

DON FERNANDO. From whom?

INSPECTOR GENERAL. The young lady on the end in the third row.

(*They spotlight the audience member with their flashlights*)

She said he ran right past her.

DON FERNANDO. I wish you well.

INSPECTOR GENERAL. I know you do, since any success I might have would also remove an obstacle for you in your quest. Come, Viceroy, I feel we are on the verge of success.

(*The* **INSPECTOR GENERAL** *and* **VICEROY** *exit into the audience, shining flashlight on the people.*)

VICEROY. Lots of wildlife out tonight. It's scaring me.

(They exit out the back. **DON FERNANDO** *exits after* **CUNEGONDE**. **CANDIDE** *and* **CACAMBO** *enter laughing with the* **QUEEN**. **CACAMBO** *eats an apple.* **CANDIDE** *drinks a latté. The* **SHEEP** *graze.)*

CACAMBO. So let me get this straight, I could take this apple, never pay for it. Meanwhile the people who grew the apple and picked the apple and brought the apple to market merrily go about their jobs of providing for me?

QUEEN. Isn't it like that everywhere?

CACAMBO. No. In Europe you can only steal the apples if you're a member of the ruling class.

QUEEN. Steal?

CANDIDE. *(whispering)* They have no concept of theft. They have no jails or laws.

(to the **QUEEN***)*

Could you get me another latté, Maybe with a pinch of chocolate, and some of that whipped cream.

QUEEN. My pleasure.

(She exits.)

CANDIDE. Amazing, isn't it.

CACAMBO. Yeah, but in a place where the dirt is gold, what do you suppose these people find valuable?

CANDIDE. Ordinary dirt, I imagine.

(They both laugh, then suddenly sober up. They pull off their shoes and empty out the accumulated dirt in their shoes.)

CACAMBO. Okay, I got about a handful.

CANDIDE. Oh, lucky. A rock! To think we used to take these for granite!

(They laugh wildly.)

CACAMBO. My, this is the best of all possible worlds!

(They freeze. The **OLD WOMAN** *walks to the center of the stage, faces the audience and speaks.)*

OLD WOMAN. One month later.

(She leaves as **CANDIDE** *and* **CACAMBO** *unfreeze. They look exceedingly bored.)*

CANDIDE. Tell me again.

CACAMBO. This is the best of all possible worlds.

CANDIDE. Oh, Cacambo, I feel so alone. Everyone I know is gone.

CACAMBO. I'm here, sir.

CANDIDE. Cunegonde, separated by mountains, Baron and Baroness, brutally butchered.

CACAMBO. He did salute you with his foot.

CANDIDE. Pangloss, hanged. Heinrich, murdered by my own hand.

CACAMBO. He *was* trying to kill you.

CANDIDE. In this best of all possible worlds, I am alone.

CACAMBO. I'm here. I've been with you from the very beginning.

CANDIDE. Why? Why?

CACAMBO. I don't know exactly. It's not as if you pay me. And you don't have any nobleman status left. And I –

CANDIDE. Why, Cunegonde, why do I have to face this world…alone?

CACAMBO. Sir, we are here in a land where the streets are paved with gold, we don't have to work, at all, and there is no crime or violence. I think we should just try and make the best of it. There are people who care for you and follow you faithfully. Shouldn't you give them some consideration, too.

CANDIDE. That's it, Cacambo. I know what to do now.

CACAMBO. You do?

CANDIDE. Yes. It's so clear. Why didn't I see it before.

CACAMBO. Well, I'm glad you finally see it. And there is something I've been meaning to reveal to you. Something…

(She starts to let down her hair to reveal her true gender.)

CANDIDE. We'll load the pink sheep with bags of jewels.

CACAMBO. What?

CANDIDE. That's what we'll do. We'll steal some animals, load them down with jewels. And after we cross the mountains, I will be the richest man in the world. Rich enough to buy Cunegonde, if I have to. Hurry Cacambo, load the animals.

CACAMBO. Me? Load the animals? What will you do?

CANDIDE. I must plan. Soon Cunegonde will be with me again.

*(**CACAMBO** reluctantly loads the **SHEEP** by stuffing wadded colored papers into their costumes. The **AMAZONS** enter.)*

QUEEN. What are you doing?

CANDIDE. We, ah…we just…

*(**CANDIDE** draws his sword.)*

Stay away! I've already killed. I'll do it again.

QUEEN. We aren't going to harm you.

CANDIDE. I'm warning you! Don't force me to do anything rash.

*(He swings the sword wildly at the **AMAZONS**.)*

We're leaving!

QUEEN. You are, by nature, free; depart whenever you please.

CANDIDE. With sheep. You heard me, a hundred sheep. And jewels.

QUEEN. Take away as much of it as you like.

CANDIDE. I'm warning you, the streets will flow with blood if you try and stop us.

QUEEN. I'm not trying to stop you.

CANDIDE. You're not?

QUEEN. No.

CANDIDE. Well, that's different, isn't it?

(awkward pause)

So.

QUEEN. So?

CANDIDE. Perhaps you could show us the way out, then.

QUEEN. There's nothing I'd rather do.

(The narrators enter along with the **HORSES** *pulling the wagon.)*

OLD WOMAN. And so the Queen of El Dorado, where all women were queens, ordered twenty beautiful virgins to help load the farm animals with jewels and golden clay.

PAQUETTE. And she ordered her engineers to build a giant crane to lift Candide, Cacambo and the loaded pack animals to the top of the cliffs.

OLD WOMAN. Never had so much energy been spent to help anyone leave El Dorado.

PAQUETTE. But then, never had anyone requested to leave El Dorado.

*(***CANDIDE** *addresses the* **AMAZONS***. The* **SHEEP** *are loaded with jewels.)*

CANDIDE. Before we go, I wish to say, we aren't thieves, and we intend to pay. Here, your majesty, divide this up among yourselves.

(He tosses her a small money bag.)

PRINCESS 1. What is it, mother?

QUEEN. A bag of dirt. Brown dirt. And a granite pebble.

PRINCESS 2. How very strange these Europeans are.

(The **AMAZONS** *moon-walk offstage to indicate the wagon is moving.* **CANDIDE, CACAMBO** *and the* **SHEEP** *bounce in the wagon to indicate a rocky road.)*

OLD WOMAN. On our travelers' first day's journey, they were elated with the prospect of being rich.

PAQUETTE. The second day two of their sheep sunk in quicksand

OLD WOMAN. Some few days afterwards seven or eight animals perished with hunger in a desert,

PAQUETTE. And others tumbled down precipices, or were otherwise lost.

OLD WOMAN. After traveling fifty days they had only four sheep left.

CACAMBO. Even so, we have still more treasure than all the Kings of Spain, England, Germany and France will ever possess....

*(A **SHEEP** dies and rolls offstage to indicate the wagon is moving away from them.)*

Spain and France will possess....

*(Another **SHEEP** dies.)*

Spain. Oh, look a town. We still have two sheep worth a fortune. We are at the end of our troubles, and the beginning of happiness.

*(The **INSPECTOR GENERAL** and **VICEROY** pop up from behind the set to intercept them. They draw pistols to cover the fugitives. **CANDIDE**, **CACAMBO** and the remaining farm animals raise their hands.)*

INSPECTOR GENERAL. You celebrate prematurely.

CANDIDE. I can offer you priceless jewels and gold.

INSPECTOR GENERAL. How perishable the riches of this world are; there is nothing solid but virtue.

CANDIDE. I thought you might say that.

INSPECTOR GENERAL. Candide, I arrest you for the murder of the Grand Inquisitor and a Banker.

VICEROY. If you will not come alive, we shall take you back the other way.

CANDIDE. So be it!

*(**CANDIDE** runs. The scene transforms into slow motion. The **HORSES** run away. The **INSPECTOR GENERAL** fires his gun. A **SPECIAL EFFECTS STAGEHAND**, dressed in black, pops up holding a large prop bullet. He flies the bullet in slow motion toward **CANDIDE**. **CACAMBO** throws himself in the air in front of the bullet. The bullet hits **CACAMBO** and ricochets off his chest. It ricochets off*

the proscenium and heads back toward the **VICEROY.** *It strikes the* **VICEROY,** *killing him, then ricochets towards the* **INSPECTOR GENERAL,** *who turns to run. The bullet finally comes to rest in the* **INSPECTOR GENERAL***'s buttock.*)

INSPECTOR GENERAL. Ow…my buttock.

(*The* **INSPECTOR GENERAL** *falls. The* **SPECIAL EFFECTS STAGEHAND** *looks both directions and then sneaks out.* **CANDIDE** *comforts the dying* **INSPECTOR GENERAL.**)

CANDIDE. Rest in peace.

INSPECTOR GENERAL. We shall never…

(*The* **INSPECTOR GENERAL** *dies before he can finish his sentence.*)

CACAMBO. Ahhhh!

(**CANDIDE** *rushes to the fallen* **CACAMBO** *and half-raises him.*)

CANDIDE. As you sink into your grave, Cacambo, remember this, Miss Cunegonde will be very glad you saved me.

CACAMBO. I'm not dead.

CANDIDE. You're not?

CACAMBO. The bullet ricocheted off a large diamond I kept close to my heart.

(**CACAMBO** *pulls a large jewel out of his shirt.* **CAN-DIDE** *seems more interested in the diamond and drops* **CACAMBO** *to examine the jewel.*)

CANDIDE. Cacambo! This may be the best of all possible worlds, after all. On to Cunegonde!

(**CANDIDE** *bounds off with the last two* **SHEEP.** **CACAMBO** *sadly follows. The dead bodies exit.*)

Scene Four

(Slide: A picture of a slave auction accompanied by the words, "Chapter Twelve: The Lawless Port of Suriname." PANGLOSS enters. He is a wreck. The noose still hangs around his neck. The butcher knife is still impaled in his chest.)

PANGLOSS. Chapter Twelve: The lawless port of Suriname. Suriname, a hot bed of thieves, pirates and murderers. And the best place to find a bargain on a used slave.

(The AUCTIONEER enters with a large crowd of buyers. HEINRICH is with them, unseen in the crowd. The AUCTIONEER whips PANGLOSS and offers him for sale.)

AUCTIONEER. What do I hear for this fine specimen.

SLAVE BUYER. He's a specimen, but I couldn't say of what.

AUCTIONEER. A perfect house slave. He speaks seven languages.

SLAVE BUYER. Seven? Who does he think he is?

PANGLOSS. I am Dr. Pangloss, foremost philosopher and teacher.

SLAVE BUYER. Doctor? By the look of you, you could use a little doctoring, yourself.

AUCTIONEER. Wait, I'll throw in this fine young lad as well. Once a priest, he can absolve you of all your sins.

(HEINRICH is pulled forward.)

PANGLOSS. Heinrich?

HEINRICH. Pangloss?

(They embrace. The butcher knife sticks HEINRICH.)

PANGLOSS. Watch the knife.

(They separate, PANGLOSS' hand falls off. HEINRICH picks it up.)

HEINRICH. This is yours.

PANGLOSS. Thanks.

(**PANGLOSS** *tries to re-attach the hand to his arm. He gives up and sticks the severed hand in his pocket. He explains to the crowd.*)

It's the syphilis.

AUCTIONEER. Look at what a strong boy this is, able to tear this other gentleman limb from limb.

HEINRICH. And handsome, too.

SLAVE BUYER. Three pence.

HEINRICH. Five pence.

SLAVE BUYER. You can't bid on yourself.

HEINRICH. But three pence is an insult.

AUCTIONEER. One of you out there must be a ship's captain. This one has a lot of work left in him. And this one, well, he can give you a hand with your chores.

(**PANGLOSS** *holds up the dismembered hand.*)

PIRATE. Three pounds.

AUCTIONEER. Sold to…

(*He sees who has bid. The* **PIRATE CAPTAIN**. *The* **AUCTIONEER** *is respectfully afeared.*)

Captain…And very generous.

PIRATE. Take them. Lock them in my galley.

HEINRICH. As in…the kitchen galley?

PIRATE. As in the galley where you row the boat until the oars blister your hands. And when your body is broken, we throw you overboard as shark bait.

HEINRICH. Oh, that galley.

PIRATE. Take them.

(*The* **AUCTIONEER** *tries to drag* **PANGLOSS** *away. His arm falls off.* **CANDIDE** *and* **CACAMBO** *enter with their* **SHEEP**.)

PANGLOSS. When Candide and Cacambo reached Suriname, they inquired after a vessel for hire.

HEINRICH. What're you doing?

PANGLOSS. I'm alive again. I can narrate if I want to. It unfolded thus.

(The **AUCTIONEER** *drags* **HEINRICH** *and* **PANGLOSS** *off.)*

CANDIDE. Is there a captain who will take us to Buenos Aires. I have gold...

(The crowd gathers round.)

There I will reunited with my fair Cunegonde...

(The crowd scatters quickly.)

Where do you go?

PIRATE. What you ask would prove our death. The fair Cunegonde is the Governor Don Fernando's favorite mistress.

*(***CANDIDE** *falls to his knees.)*

CANDIDE. Noooooo!

*(***CUNEGONDE,** *the* **OLD WOMAN,** *and* **PAQUETTE** *pop up from behind the scenery. They hear the "Nooooo." and look confused.* **CUNEGONDE** *now wears layers of jewels around her neck.)*

PAQUETTE. What was that?

CUNEGONDE. I didn't hear anything.

OLD WOMAN. I have one buttock.

(The three women sink slowly below the platform level. The **PIRATE** *exits.* **CACAMBO** *helps* **CANDIDE** *up.)*

CACAMBO. Maybe now we can go back to Europe and remember Miss Cunegonde the way –

CANDIDE. I have it. You have five or six millions in diamonds in your pockets. Go to Buenos Aires and buy her back. As you have not killed an Inquisitor, they will have no reason to hold you. I'll fit out another ship and go to Venice, where I will wait for Cunegonde.

CACAMBO. You want me to travel to Buenos Aires?

CANDIDE. Yes.

CACAMBO. Buy Miss Cunegonde with *my* diamonds?

CANDIDE. Yes.

CACAMBO. And meet you in Venice?

CANDIDE. Venice is a free country where we shall have nothing to fear.

CACAMBO. Who will tend to your needs?

CANDIDE. Oh, I'll pick up another serving person here in Port.

(**CACAMBO** *is hurt and starts to slink off.*)

Wait...

(**CANDIDE** *moves to* **CACAMBO**. *He takes the large jewel that deflected the bullet out of* **CACAMBO**'s *pocket.*)

I'll offer this to your replacement to assure I hire the best man....

(**CACAMBO** *runs off.* **CANDIDE** *asks the audience.*)

What?

(**PAQUETTE** *and the* **OLD WOMAN** *lead* **MARTIN** *the hyperactive pessimist on stage. His manic but sour mood is infectious.*)

PAQUETTE. Enter Martin, a servant.

OLD WOMAN. Full name? Martin the pessimist.

MARTIN. It's a little late in the play to add a main character, isn't it?

PAQUETTE. Perhaps you're not a main character.

MARTIN. That's my first complaint, then.

OLD WOMAN. Martin was a poor scholar, who had been robbed by his wife,

PAQUETTE. Beaten by his son,

OLD WOMAN. And forsaken by his daughter.

MARTIN. Life sucks, doesn't it?

CANDIDE. See to the sheep, Martin, while I find us passage on a ship.

MARTIN. What am I? Your servant?

CANDIDE. Technically, yes.

MARTIN. Well, just shoot me.

(The **PIRATE CAPTAIN** *re-enters.)*

CANDIDE. Captain, what will you charge to carry us directly to Venice?

PIRATE. Venice? Why I'd be a fool to take you there for less than ten thousand piastres.

CANDIDE. Done. When can we leave.

PIRATE. Never. I never said I would take you for ten thousand. I only said I would be a fool to take you for less. A fair price is twenty-thousand piastres.

CANDIDE. Very well, twenty-thousand piastres.

PIRATE. *(aside to audience)* Zounds! This man will pay twenty thousand piastres with as much ease as ten.

(to **CANDIDE***)*

Sir, a fair price *is* twenty thousand, but did I say I was a fair man? No, I am unfair. Therefore, my price is thirty thousand Piastres…and…a thousand hot pockets.

CANDIDE. You shall have it.

PIRATE. *(aside)* Thirty thousand! Those sheep must be laden with…

*(***CANDIDE** *is looking over his shoulder listening.)*

Deal. Have your livestock brought aboard immediately. We sail in the morning.

(The **PIRATE** *goes to his own cartoonishly cardboard ship to wait.)*

MARTIN. That went badly.

CANDIDE. Very well, I think.

MARTIN. Well, you're a loon, then.

CANDIDE. Just take the sheep on board.

MARTIN. I will, but only to prove you wrong. Watch. I take the sheep on board.

(He forces the **SHEEP** *onto the ship with the* **PIRATE***.)*

We go off to get ready.

(He pulls **CANDIDE** *aside.)*

The ship sails away.

CANDIDE. Why would you think that?

MARTIN. Maybe it's the flag they're flying.

(The ship sails away flying a skull and crossed bones. **MARTIN** *waves at the* **PIRATE**.*)*

Bon Voyage.

PIRATE. *(calling back as he exits with the* **SHEEP**) You were so trusting, I feel bad – almost.

MARTIN. Have a good trip.

*(***CANDIDE** *falls on the ground and opens his mouth to let out a silent "Nooooo."* **CUNEGONDE**, *the* **OLD WOMAN**, *and* **PAQUETTE** *pop up from behind the scenery.* **CUNEGONDE** *now wears an insane amount of bejeweled bling. The women listen, but since it is a silent scream, they can hear nothing. They shrug and sink slowly back behind the platforms.)*

MARTIN. I see you are speechless.

CANDIDE. I nearly find myself, after all, obliged to renounce Optimism.

MARTIN. Optimism is merely maintaining that everything is best when it is worst.

CANDIDE. And what is your pessimism?

MARTIN. Reality. You've lost everything.

CANDIDE. Everything. Except of course, these jewels…

(He pulls jewels out of his shirt.)

And bags of gold that I have in my pockets. But they can't be worth more than five or six million.

(The **OLD WOMAN** *enters.)*

OLD WOMAN. More cautiously, Candide booked passage on a ship heading for France.

Scene Five

(Slide: A ship at sea accompanied by the words, "Chapter Thirteen: How Candide was Forced to Listen to His New Teacher, Martin, the Pessimist." **MARTIN** *and* **CANDIDE** *take up residence on the ship.)*

OLD WOMAN. Chapter Thirteen: How Candide was forced to listen to his new teacher, Martin, the pessimist.

(She exits.)

MARTIN. I must confess, when I cast my eye on this world, I cannot help thinking that God has abandoned it to the devil.

CANDIDE. You're jesting.

MARTIN. Jesting? Is there a city that does not wish the destruction of its neighboring city; a family that does not desire to exterminate some other family?

CANDIDE. Thank you, Martin. That's quite enough pessimism for one day.

MARTIN. I've barely started. The poor hate the rich, even while they creep and cringe to them.

CANDIDE. That's very negative.

MARTIN. And the rich treat the poor like sheep!

CANDIDE. Only fourteen more days 'til France.

*(***PAQUETTE*** enters with some* **SPECIAL EFFECTS HELPERS** *who unfold long strips of blue material that stretch nearly from wing to wing. They ripple the fabric like waves in the ocean.)*

PAQUETTE. This might have gone on forever except this happened.

*(***CANDIDE*** points into the waves of fabric. Dead people float by, or rather, actors pretending to be dead bodies inch through the blue fabric.)*

CANDIDE. Look!

MARTIN. What? It's debris from a shipwreck.

CANDIDE. Look! My faith and optimism is restored.

MARTIN. By a shipwreck?

CANDIDE. Not a shipwreck. Look!

(*The* **PIRATE SKIPPER** *floats by drowning.*)

PIRATE. Help. I'm drowning.

MARTIN. It's that pirate skipper.

PIRATE. I'm drowning. I'm drowning. I'm…dead.

MARTIN. I grant you, perhaps this pirate has met the fate he deserved. But why should the other passengers be doomed as well? God punished the pirate, and the Devil drowned the rest.

CANDIDE. No, Look!

(*A* **SHEEP** *floats on stage.*)

MARTIN. A sheep?

CANDIDE. Not *a* sheep. *My* sheep.

MARTIN. That restores your faith and optimism? A sheep?

CANDIDE. My sheep.

(**CANDIDE** *pulls the* **SHEEP** *on board.*)

MARTIN. But one of the sheep drowned.

CANDIDE. But one survived.

MARTIN. But one drowned.

CANDIDE. But one survived.

MARTIN. But one drowned.

CANDIDE. But one survived.

MARTIN. But one…

CANDIDE. Look!

(**HEINRICH** *and* **PANGLOSS** *float on stage, clinging to the other* **SHEEP**. *Along with the noose and butcher knife and tin nose,* **PANGLOSS** *now carries his severed limb. Candide helps all aboard. Everybody hugs.*)

Pangloss! Heinrich! Fluffy!

PANGLOSS. Oooh, watch the knife.

HEINRICH. Brother.

CANDIDE. I am so happy to rescue you, having only recently killed you.

HEINRICH. No happier than I.

MARTIN. Is this not strange to you?

CANDIDE. What?

MARTIN. Don't you find it strange that these people who were dead are now alive and standing before you?

ALL. No. Not really. Do you think it's strange? No. I've seen stranger. Baaaa. etc.

MARTIN. Don't you even want to hear their stories? How they were turned into galley slaves?

HEINRICH. Things happened.

PANGLOSS. And now it's all for the best.

HEINRICH. Because, here we are.

MARTIN. That's no answer.

CANDIDE. All right. Sum it up, in one sentence.

HEINRICH. I did not know it was a crime for a Christian to be found naked in a bath with a young Turk.

CANDIDE. Good. And you?

PANGLOSS. A very pretty young female had, in her bosom, a beautiful nosegay of tulips, roses, and hyacinths.

CANDIDE. And you?

BOTH SHEEP. Baaaa.

CANDIDE. Satisfied?

MARTIN. Never.

CANDIDE. And if we can reunite, then there's a chance I can fulfill my vow and find the fair Cunegonde.

MARTIN. A chance? Are you serious?

CANDIDE. Yes.

MARTIN. You gave your *servant* six million in jewels and said, "Go get Cunegonde, and when you get back, you'll have the honor of being my servant again."

CANDIDE. Cacambo is an honest fellow.

MARTIN. As honest as any, but he's sitting somewhere on a beach, counting his money and sipping a pina colada. And who's that at his side? His new wife Cunegonde!

*(They all laugh at **MARTIN**.)*

HEINRICH. My, he *is* a pessimist.

(*They laugh again. The special effects leave as* **PAQUETTE** *and* **OLD WOMAN** *enter.*)

PAQUETTE. Thus, Candide was reunited with his boyhood countrymen.

OLD WOMAN. Soon the ship neared the port of Bordeaux, France, and...

(**MARTIN** *steps off the ship and talks to the narrators.*)

MARTIN. I just wish you could've sent us anywhere but France. We're trying to get to Venice, for heaven's sake.

PAQUETTE. In the book they travel next to France.

MARTIN. Like you're following the book.

OLD WOMAN. In spirit.

MARTIN. You could've sent us to Holland. I like the people in Holland. They're a bunch of accountants and stuff, who have the good sense to stay inside and be miserable.

PAQUETTE. What's wrong with France.

MARTIN. Their ruling passion is love, the next to talk nonsense and slander. Well, at least you're not sending us to Paris.

HEINRICH. What's in Paris?

MARTIN. It's chaos. Everyone seeks pleasure without being able to find it.

PANGLOSS. What kind of pleasure.

MARTIN. Gluttony, Can-Can dancers, Casinos, Ladies of the evening. But who wants that?

(**HEINRICH, PANGLOSS** *and the* **SHEEP** *raise their hands.*)

ALL. Me. Baa. etc.

CANDIDE. For my part, I desire to behold nothing except Miss Cunegonde, but...I mean, how many chances do you get to see Paris?

Scene Six

(Slide: a picture of can-can dancers accompanied by the words, "Chapter Thirteen and a Half: Paris, the City of Love.")

OLD WOMAN. And so after landing in Bordeaux, our hero…

MARTIN. Here, let me narrate this one.

OLD WOMAN. But…

MARTIN. Yes, we all know. One butt.

*(The **OLD WOMAN** and **PAQUETTE** exit.)*

Chapter Thirteen and a Half: They went to France. Paris. But it wouldn't make them happy.

*(Scurvy people come out to greet **CANDIDE**'s entourage. Even the **SHEEP** are scared.)*

HEINRICH. My, this *is* vile.

MARTIN. Of course it is. They entered the city by the suburbs of Saint-Marceau, known as a hangout for pickpockets, sharpies, and…and…mimes.

*(They are approached by a young street mime, **RATTOLI**. She mimes the words in parenthesis.)*

RATTOLI. (Want to buy a watch?)

PANGLOSS. Let me translate. One of my seven languages is mime.

(He watches her pantomime again.)

My dear, I don't think wrist watches are invented yet.

RATTOLI. (How about some postcards?)

*(She hands **PANGLOSS** postcards, shocking postcards.)*

PANGLOSS. She wants us to look at postcards. Paris is known for her artists.

(He realizes the subject matter.)

Ahh!

HEINRICH. Let me see.

(He takes the postcards.)

Ahh!

(CANDIDE is passed cards but doesn't seem to know what he is looking at. He twists the cards and skews his head to get a different angle.)

CANDIDE. Hummm?

MARTIN. It was a vile place.

RATTOLI. (Hey, be careful with those....)

(In taking back the postcards, RATTOLI notices a big diamond ring on CANDIDE's hand. RATTOLI instinctively tries to wrench the ring off of CANDIDE's finger.)

CANDIDE. Excuse me.

RATTOLI. *(calming her excitement)* (Is it real?)

PANGLOSS. She asks if it's real.

CANDIDE. I only know that this is just as real as these.

(CANDIDE pulls handfulls of jewels out of his pockets.)

RATTOLI. (What is your wildest dream?)

PANGLOSS. She wants to know your wildest fantasy.

CANDIDE. I was thinking, visit the Opera house. Maybe the Ballet.

RATTOLI. (No.)

CANDIDE. No?

RATTOLI. (You are men. You have come to see Paris. Not be some sissy boys at the ballet.)

(She leads them all in laughter, although hers is silent.)

MARTIN. Laugh away. The people of Paris are always laughing, and commit the most detestable crimes with a smile on their faces.

RATTOLI. (Who is this?)

PANGLOSS. Martin, the pessimist.

RATTOLI. (Is he going to spoil all our fun?)

PANGLOSS. Oh, yes. He dislikes to see anyone having fun.

MARTIN. The mime led them past opium dens, past bordellos, past, I hate to say it...theaters, to a part of town where....

(*TWO* **POLICEMEN** *sneak up behind* **MARTIN** *and conk him on the head.* **RATTOLI** *leads the group offstage. The* **MADAME** *enters and picks up the narration mid-sentence.*)

MADAME. Where they were suddenly separated from Martin, the pessimist.

(*to* **POLICEMEN**)

Take him to the judge. Thirty days in the Bastille should cure him.

(*The* **POLICEMEN** *laugh like Frenchmen as they drag* **MARTIN** *off.*)

Enter Mademoiselle Clairon, A Business woman. This is my casino...

(**RATTOLI** *leads the group on stage.*)

Welcome to my house.

ALL. (*ad libbing*) Nice place...Very friendly...Baaa...etc.

(**MADAME** *pulls* **RATTOLI** *aside.*)

MADAME. What have you brought me?

RATTOLI. (*speaking*) Candide, a nobleman, at the very least.

MADAME. How do you know?

RATTOLI. He paid me with this.

(*She shows* **MADAME** *a large jewel.*)

One claims to be a Baron, the other the greatest philosopher in Europe.

MADAME. And the sheep?

RATTOLI. Pets.

MADAME. Any money?

RATTOLI. No. They're just sheep.

MADAME. I mean, do the men have money.

RATTOLI. Candide's the one. On the way here he bragged of his unrequited love for a baroness.

MADAME. I have ways to quiet a man's feelings.

(They laugh. **PANGLOSS** *and* **HEINRICH** *come in and looks over their shoulders.* **RATTOLI** *becomes a mime again.)*

HEINRICH. Why do you laugh?

MADAME. Monsieurs, we laugh because the rules of probability have been suspended tonight. At the roulette wheel, at the card table, at the baccarat, winner after winner is paid.

HEINRICH. Then why are you laughing.

MADAME. It is only money. And it makes the customers so happy.

HEINRICH. Roulette. I've always heard of that game.

MADAME. And may I suggest the numbers 27 is very lucky today.

*(***HEINRICH*** begs* **CANDIDE** *for a stake.)*

HEINRICH. Please? The laws of probability are suspended.

*(***RATTOLI*** begs with him.)*

CANDIDE. Alright.

*(***CANDIDE*** gives* **HEINRICH** *a jewel. He runs off with* **RATTOLI** *to play roulette.)*

MADAME. *(to* **PANGLOSS***)* Perhaps you would like a more relaxing activity?

PANGLOSS. I must admit, I prefer talk to gambling.

MADAME. These ladies, also, enjoy a good debate. Meet Mimi and Youyou.

(Two of the **MADAME***'s employees enter.)*

MIMI. Hello Sailor, I bet you have some interesting stories.

PANGLOSS. Actually, I'm more of a galley slave than a sailor.

YOUYOU. Then you're acquainted with handcuffs and whips?

PANGLOSS. As well as nooses and scalpels.

MIMI. Such knowledge may come in handy.

PANGLOSS. That has always been my philosophy.

YOUYOU. How did you lose that cute little nose?

PANGLOSS. A fast acting, highly contagious, venereal disease.

*(All three laugh like Frenchmen. **PANGLOSS**' arm falls off. They laugh harder. They exit, leaving **CANDIDE** and the **MADAME** alone except for the **SHEEP**.)*

MADAME. They tell me you have a fiancee.

CANDIDE. Miss Cunegonde, the most beautiful girl in all Westphalia.

MADAME. You answer me like a boy;

CANDIDE. Do I?

MADAME. A Frenchman would say, 'It is true, Madame, I had a great passion for Miss Cunegonde; but since I have seen you, I fear I can no longer love her as I did.'"

CANDIDE. He would?

MADAME. You fell in love with her stooping to pick up a handkerchief which she dropped?

CANDIDE. Yes.

MADAME. Now…you shall pick up my garter.

*(She undoes a garter from her leg and drops it in front of **CANDIDE**. He looks confused.)*

Well, pick it up.

(He picks it up and holds it out, but she doesn't take it.)

But you must put it on.

CANDIDE. All right.

(He starts to put it on his own leg.)

MADAME. Not on you. Put it on me.

(He tries, but is too shy to touch her leg.)

CANDIDE. I can't.

(She grabs him.)

MADAME. I make some of my lovers here in Paris languish a whole month;

CANDIDE. What are you doing?

MADAME. But I surrender to you at first sight, to do the honors of my country to a young Westphalian.

(She wrestles a kiss out of him. They roll off the back edge of the platform. Only the **SHEEP** *are left on stage. They peer over the back edge of the platform where* **CANDIDE** *and the* **MADAME** *wrestle unseen.)*

SHEEP 1. Baaaa.

(The **POLICEMEN** *enter, dragging* **HEINRICH** *behind them.)*

HEINRICH. Excuse me…

*(***CANDIDE** *pops up from behind the platform.)*

I need a few more jewels.

CANDIDE. What?

HEINRICH. Five… maybe ten.

CANDIDE. I can't afford to stake you to anymore.

HEINRICH. Well, it isn't a stake so much as… paying my tab.

CANDIDE. Your tab?

HEINRICH. They're taking me to jail.

CANDIDE. Here….

(He starts to take off his diamond ring but notices it is no longer on his finger. All his bling is gone.)

Hey!

*(***MADAME** *stands up. She admires the ring on her own finger as she exits laughing.)*

HEINRICH. I don't know what happened. I was winning. Then, all of a sudden, my luck changed.

*(***CANDIDE** *grudgingly gives him some jewels from his pocket.)*

One more. The big one.

*(***CANDIDE** *gives it. The* **POLICEMEN** *carry* **HEINRICH** *off.* **RATTOLI** *enters carrying a letter.)*

RATTOLI. *(miming)* (A letter for you.)

CANDIDE. A letter?

(**RATTOLI** *shrugs. She uses a pantomime rope to pull* **FLASHBACK CUNEGONDE** *on stage as* **CANDIDE** *opens the letter.*)

FLASHBACK CUNEGONDE. *(writing)* My Dearest Lover –

CANDIDE. It's from Cunegonde.

(**RATTOLI** *nods. She runs off.* **CANDIDE** *talks to the* **SHEEP.**)

FLASHBACK CUNEGONDE. I have been ill in this city these eight days.

CANDIDE. She's ill?

FLASHBACK CUNEGONDE. I have heard of your arrival, and should fly to your arms were I able to stir.

CANDIDE. My goodness, she's unable to stir.

FLASHBACK CUNEGONDE. The Governor of Buenos Aires has taken everything from me...

CANDIDE. What?

FLASHBACK CUNEGONDE. But your heart, which I still retain.

(*The* **SHEEP** *give* **CANDIDE** *a little "ah, shucks" punch on the shoulder.*)

CANDIDE. Wait, there's more.

FLASHBACK CUNEGONDE. Come to me immediately. You will give me new life, but if you do not come, I die.

CANDIDE. And here's the address. Cunegonde, I am on my way.

(**CANDIDE** *exuberantly exits.*)

FLASHBACK CUNEGONDE. P.S....

(**CANDIDE** *rushs back.*)

FLASHBACK CUNEGONDE. Bring all your wealth. All your wealth.

(**CANDIDE** *exits with the* **SHEEP**. **PAQUETTE** *and the* **OLD WOMAN** *enter. They carry a wide, floor-length curtain between them on a pole. The curtain is split in the middle, but traversed closed so the audience cannot see what is behind it.*)

OLD WOMAN. He took his gold and his jewels and proceeded to the house where Miss Cunegonde lodged.

(**CANDIDE** *rushes on with all his wealth.*)

PAQUETTE. Upon entering the room he felt his limbs tremble,

OLD WOMAN. His heart flutter,

PAQUETTE. His tongue falter;

(**CANDIDE** *calls to the other side of the curtain.*)

CANDIDE. Yoo-hoo. Cunegonde.

POLICEMAN 1. (*He is unseen behind the curtain and speaks with a woman's voice.*) Sir, don't open the curtains Miss Chupacabra cannot bear the least light.

CANDIDE. Who?

POLICEMAN 1. (*unseen*) My Lady is sensitive to the light.

(*An arm comes through the slit in the curtain and beckons* **CANDIDE** *to it.*)

CANDIDE. Cunegonde! Is that you? Speak to me.

POLICEMAN 1. (*unseen*) Alas! she cannot speak.

POLICEMAN 2. (*unseen*)

(*behind curtain with a woman's voice*)

It's my illness.

CANDIDE. You sound different.

POLICEMAN 2. (*unseen*) Take my hand, Candide.

(*He takes her hand and starts to kiss it. He stops abruptly, noticing her arm is muscular and hairy.*)

CANDIDE. Your arm? Swollen. Twice its size. Oh, what illness could –

POLICEMAN 2. (*unseen*) Did you bring the jewels, my little apple strudel?

CANDIDE. What? Yes, of course.

POLICEMAN 2. (*unseen*)

(*male voice*)

Good.

(POLICEMEN 2 pulls CANDIDE in through the curtain. We hear the sounds of a struggle. Billy clubs rise and fall over the top of the curtain. Wads of jewels fly up high in the air. CANDIDE crawls out under the curtain. Before he can escape he is dragged back behind the curtain, legs first. Pieces of clothing fly in the air. PAQUETTE and the OLD WOMAN peer behind themselves over the top of the curtain. They shake their heads.)

PAQUETTE. *(to OLD WOMAN)* Anything to narrate here?

OLD WOMAN. No. Pretty self-explanatory.

(They walk the curtain off the stage. When the curtain exits, CANDIDE is alone on stage, hurt and disheveled. HEINRICH flies on stage, as if launched from a trampoline, and rolls to a stop next to CANDIDE. PANGLOSS's arm flies in next and the old man follows it. The SHEEP launch in next. Their pink ribbons are missing.)

CANDIDE. Monsters.

SHEEP. Baaaa.

HEINRICH. How much money do we have left?

CANDIDE. Nothing.

PANGLOSS. If it's any consolation, how could things get worse?

(MARTIN launches in from the wings. He lands and rolls across the width of the stage. Turning over and over long after his momentum should have stopped.)

HEINRICH. You should never say that.

CANDIDE. They let you go?

MARTIN. When you lost your wealth, I was no more use to them.

CANDIDE. I see.

MARTIN. Or it may have been, they couldn't stand me anymore.

(PAQUETTE enters.)

PAQUETTE. As they sat there wallowing in their despair, the travelers were approached by a friendly lady of the night.

(**PAQUETTE** *addresses the men strewn about the stage.*)

Hey sailors.

HEINRICH. Sorry, we are all out of money.

PANGLOSS. Wait! I recognize that voice.

HEINRICH. Of course. It was mine.

PANGLOSS. Not yours. Hers. Paquette!

(*He jumps up and rushes to* **PAQUETTE** *to give her a one-armed hug.*)

PAQUETTE. Pangloss? You're looking...alive...Heinie?

HEINRICH. *(still very nervous around her)* L-l-l-long time no pee. See. No see.

CANDIDE. Paquette? Oh, tell me, is Cunegonde with you?

PAQUETTE. Alas, no.

CANDIDE. Of course. She's waiting in a Palace in Venice purchased by Cacambo with my jewels.

PAQUETTE. There's no palace.

CANDIDE. But I gave him millions.

PAQUETTE. He was obliged to buy her from Seignor Don Fernando.

FLASHBACK DON FERNANDO. *(entering with the flashback versions of* **CUNEGONDE, CACAMBO, PAQUETTE** *and* **OLD WOMAN**) Don Fernando d'Ibaraa y Figueora y Mascarenes y Lampourdos y Souza de Cucarocha.

FLASHBACK CACAMBO. I will offer you 10,000 in gold for the lot.

FLASHBACK CUNEGONDE. I, alone, am worth ten times ten thousand. Name your price, governor.

CANDIDE. Flashback Cunegonde. I don't trust her.

FLASHBACK DON FERNANDO. Two-million...in gold.

FLASHBACK CACAMBO. Sold.

(*The flashback characters exit.*)

CANDIDE. What? Cacambo didn't even try and bargain.

PAQUETTE. To compound the problem, Cacambo booked passage on a pirate ship.

MARTIN. Only an idiot would book passage on a pirate ship.

PAQUETTE. That's what I said.

CANDIDE. Go on.

PAQUETTE. Halfway to Venice, the Pirates took all our money and set Cacambo, Cunegonde, and the Old Woman with One Buttock adrift in a leaky rowboat.

PANGLOSS. And yourself?

PAQUETTE. I was kept on board, obliged to continue the abominable trade which you men think so pleasing, but which to us unhappy creatures is the most dreadful of all sufferings.

PANGLOSS. You mean…high school teacher?

PAQUETTE. No. The very trade which I now ply.

HEINRICH. Oh? Oh!

PAQUETTE. At length I came to follow the business to Paris. Ah! sirs, to be obliged to receive every visitor; old tradesman, counselor –

CANDIDE. Enough of you. What about Cunegonde?

PAQUETTE. Cunegonde is long since drowned.

(**CANDIDE** *collapses.*)

CANDIDE. Pangloss, when you were hanged, dissected, whipped, and tugging at the oar, did you continue to think that everything in this world happens for the best?

PANGLOSS. I am a philosopher, and it would do me no good to deny my principles.

CANDIDE. Well, you are wrong…and Martin is right; all is misery and deceit.

(*He stands up and moves center for dramatic effect.*)

Here and now….I disavow…forever…the philosophy of –

CACAMBO. Master.

(**CACAMBO** *enters. The* **OLD WOMAN** *follows him with* **CUNEGONDE** *who wears a veil over her face. She is dressed like a beggar and walks with a stoop.*)

CANDIDE. Cacambo?

CACAMBO. I have returned –

CANDIDE. Where is Cunegonde.

(**CANDIDE** *rushes right past* **CACAMBO** *to look for* **CUNEGONDE.** *She is there, but* **CANDIDE** *does not recognize her in her shabby state. He turns and rushes back to* **CACAMBO.**)

Where is she.

CUNEGONDE. Here, my love.

(*He hears the voice behind him and brightens.* **CUNEGONDE** *removes her veil to reveal she has grown incredibly ugly.*)

I'm here.

(**CANDIDE** *turns and rushes to the voice.*)

CANDIDE. My –

(*He realizes she is now ugly and pulls up.*)

Whoa….

(**CANDIDE** *draws the* **OLD WOMAN** *aside, thinking it is* **CACAMBO.**)

Cacambo, what…..

(*He tosses the* **OLD WOMAN** *away and goes to get the real* **CACAMBO** *for an aside.*)

Cacambo, what happened to Cunegonde?

CACAMBO. Well, master, she has grown incredibly ugly.

CANDIDE. I can see that.

CACAMBO. We were out at sea, no shelter from the blistering sun.

OLD WOMAN. The tender Candide, upon seeing his fair Cunegonde all sunburned.

PAQUETTE. With bleary eyes.

OLD WOMAN. A withered neck.

PAQUETTE. Wrinkled face and arms.

OLD WOMAN. All covered with a red scurf –

CANDIDE. Stop narrating!

*(There is a pause as **CANDIDE** collects himself.)*

PAQUETTE. *(whispering)* Recovering himself, he advanced towards her out of good manners.

CANDIDE. Shhhh!

OLD WOMAN. *(whispering.)* Cunegonde, not knowing that she had grown ugly, as no one had informed her of it, reminded Candide of his promise.

CUNEGONDE. Now we can be married.

CANDIDE. What?

HEINRICH. What?

CUNEGONDE. Nothing stands in our way, now.

HEINRICH. Married? To Candide? I will never allow it!

CUNEGONDE. Brother, does my happiness mean so little?

CANDIDE. Cunegonde, he is entitled to his opinion.

HEINRICH. No sister of mine shall ever be the wife of any person below the rank of Baron of the Empire.

CUNEGONDE. What Empire is left?

CANDIDE. We should listen to both sides here.

MARTIN. *(to **CANDIDE**)* Get a sword. Just kill him again.

HEINRICH. Thou mayest kill me again, but thou shalt not marry my sister while I am living.

CANDIDE. What a dilemma.

CUNEGONDE. Candide?

CANDIDE. I'm just saying, your brother has a point.

(He turns away from her to think.)

CUNEGONDE. Was it only my looks that attracted you? Was all this journey, then, for some superficial notion of perfection?

*(**CANDIDE** does not answer.)*

Was it nothing but physics and Newton's laws of motion and a series of bad puns? Did you mean a word you said?

CANDIDE. I meant everything, at the time.

CUNEGONDE. Is all your optimism gone?

(He shrugs.)

There are two philosophies here. One leads step by step toward happiness. The other is instant hopelessness and despair.

CANDIDE. What if pessimism is the truth?

CUNEGONDE. It can't be. A philosophy isn't true or false. You choose what to believe in...We can be happy, Candide.

CANDIDE. Can we? This is the grand question, isn't it. Which is worst,

(He points to PAQUETTE.)

to be ravished a hundred times by pirates,

(to the OLD WOMAN)

to have one buttock cut off,

(to PANGLOSS)

to be whipped and hanged,

(to HEINRICH)

to be sold into slavery and killed by your brother,

(to SHEEP)

to be cast as a sheep,

(The SHEEP shrug.)

to experience all the miseries through which every one of us hath passed following a life of adventure, or is it worse to now pursue a simple life?

CUNEGONDE. Dr. Pangloss. What is optimism?

PANGLOSS. Everything is for the best in the best of all possible worlds.

CUNEGONDE. No. Optimism is a farmer planting a seed, and watering the seed, and trusting that, somewhere down the road, it will grow...I will become beautiful again in time...

(Everyone on stage shakes their head "No.")

CUNEGONDE. *(cont.)* Or not. But we'll remember the time when I dropped my handkerchief, and you reacted. Happiness is a sum of events. It's not an event.

*(***CANDIDE*** *looks to* ***PANGLOSS***.)*

PANGLOSS. This way to happiness.

*(***CANDIDE*** *looks to* ***MARTIN***.)*

MARTIN. This way to despair…No waiting.

CANDIDE. I choose…to believe in Cunegonde.

(Group hug. Even the ***SHEEP*** *Get a hug.)*

And Cunegonde, I don't care how ugly you've become. And…what's this?

*(***CANDIDE*** *finds a large jewel buried in the wool of a* ***SHEEP***.)*

Caught in the wool? A jewel! A big one! I will use this jewel to buy a piece of land. Yes! For all of us.

SHEEP. Baaaa.

CANDIDE. And farm animals. And on that land we will plant a garden. And it will be the garden…of Eden. We will grow cabbage, and lintels, and green beans, and cumquats, and cauliflower and truffles, and we will work the land, for what could be more optimistic than to plant a seed and trust that it will grow.

Scene Seven

*(Slide: A picture of a garden, accompanied by the words,
"Chapter Fourteen: In Conclusion." An apple flies
in from the wings and* **PANGLOSS** *catches it.)*

PANGLOSS. Chapter Fourteen: In conclusion – I think I
won.

MARTIN. Damn.

PANGLOSS. The little piece of ground yielded them a plentiful crop.

CUNEGONDE. Cunegonde indeed was very ugly, but she
became an excellent hand at pastry work.

CANDIDE. She and Candide learned that happiness was
something earned by the repetition of simple actions.

HEINRICH. Heinrich, no longer a Baron, turned out to be a
very good carpenter, and became an honest man.

PAQUETTE. Making Paquette an honest woman.

CACAMBO. Cacambo revealed that she was not Cacambo
the loyal manservant, but Rosalind, daughter of Duke
Senior of Arden and left to be in another play where
she could have the lead.

OLD WOMAN. The old woman relayed her stories to the
sheep, who did not seem to mind no matter how many
times she told them.

MARTIN. Martin died rather than turn an optimist.

SHEEP 1. And every morning, all would gather to listen to
the old teacher Pangloss.

SHEEP 2. Sometimes he would speak like this.

PANGLOSS. There is an interconnection of all events in the
best of possible worlds; for, in short, had you not been
kicked out of a fine castle for the love of Miss Cunegonde;

(The **BARON** *and* **BARONESS** *run on and strike a pose.)*

had the Bulgarians not attacked,

(The **BULGARIAN ARMY** *rushes on stage with swords
drawn and strikes a pose.)*

PANGLOSS. *(cont.)* had I not been hanged and others murdered,

> *(The* **EXECUTIONERS**, **DON ISSACHAR** *and the* **GRAND INQUISITOR** *come out and wave.)*

had there not been an America, both good and bad,

> *(***DON FERNANDO** *enters on one side, the* **AMAZONS** *on the other.)*

had Pirates not stolen half your wealth,

> *(The* **PIRATES** *ARRRGGGHHH onto stage.)*

and Parisians finished the task

> *(The Parisians enter laughing.)*

and had not all this been for the best...we would not have been here, now...to eat...this...apple.

> *(He tosses the apple into the air. The* **PIRATE SKIPPER** *steps in and intercepts the apple before it returns to* **PANGLOSS**.*)*

PIRATE. Wait. That's it? That's the ending?

PANGLOSS. Yes.

MADAME. But you promised us you would tell us the meaning of life.

PANGLOSS. That is the meaning of life. "The little piece of ground yielded them a plentiful crop."

AMAZON QUEEN. The meaning of life is "plant a garden?" Just, "plant a garden?"

PANGLOSS. As it was in the Garden of Eden.

EXECUTIONER 1. That's rather anticlimactic, isn't it?

ALL. Yeah!

PANGLOSS. That's what it says in the book.

DON FERNANDO. Wait a minute! You said we weren't doing Voltaire's *Candide*.

ISSACHAR. That's right. You said we were doing the Westphalia Community Players' *Candide*.

PANGLOSS. Well, what exactly do you suggest?

GRAND INQUISITOR. Maybe something a little more heroic.

PANGLOSS. Like?

(The **INSPECTOR GENERAL** *and* **VICEROY,** *appear at the back of the house.)*

INSPECTOR GENERAL. I am here, Candide.

(He runs down the aisle and leaps up on stage. He has one buttock. The **VICEROY** *dutifully follows onto the stage.)*

And we will not rest until justice is served!

(There is a beat. Then everyone breaks into war. Slow motion killing and fighting accompanied by heroic music. **CANDIDE** *and* **CUNEGONDE** *and the three narrators walk to the apron, dodging combatants, as the curtain slowly closes on the violence behind them.)*

PANGLOSS. Human grandeur is very dangerous, if we believe the testimonies of almost all philosophers.

PAQUETTE. And so Candide and Cunegonde lived out the rest of their lives in simple pursuits.

OLD WOMAN. Working day after day, planting, sowing, a lot in life preferable to that of Kings.

PANGLOSS. Side by side, on a little patch of earth.

CANDIDE & CUNEGONDE. Cultivating happiness.

The End

PROP LIST

PROLOGUE
  Character sign: Voltaire
  Character Sign: Franklin

CHAPTER ONE: WESTPHALIA
  Three Plastic babies (to fly in from wings)
  An apple
  A hand mirror
  Paper and pencil for students and farm animals
  Cunegonde's handkerchief (no blood)
  Suitcases
  Candide's assorted worldly possessions

CHAPTER TWO: AMONG THE BULGARIANS
  Deserter uniform
  Wallet with picture of mom
  Plastic guns for Bulgarian officers
  Assorted weapons for Bulgarian soldiers (plastic swords, etc.)
  Improvised weapons for Westphalia's army (fly swatters, toilet plungers, etc.)
  Cunegonde's bloody handkerchief
  Bulgarian Soldier's prop head
  Severed limbs (an assortment)

CHAPTER THREE: THE BATTLEFIELD
  Tin nose
  Character Sign: Columbus

CHAPTER FOUR: AT SEA, TO PORTUGAL
  Two-piece, Cartoonish Boat

CHAPTER FIVE: LISBON
  Styrofoam Rocks
  Stake with fire curtain: to be burned at.
  A Charred skeleton
  Rope for a noose
  Three Veils
  A flogging whip

CHAPTER SIX: CUNEGONDE'S HIDEAWAY
  Character Sign: Flashback Cunegonde
  Character Sign: Flashback Heinrich
  Character Sign: Flashback Baron

Character Sign: Flashback Don Issachar
Jewels for Cunegonde: necklaces, rings, bracelets, etc.
Character Sign: Flashback Old Woman
Character Sign: Flashback Paquette
Character Sign: Flashback Grand Inquisitor
Don Isachar's gift box and jewelry contents
Sword
Ballet Tutu
Grand Inquisitor's gift box and present

CHAPTER SEVEN: CADIZ, OR THEREABOUTS (MEANWHILE)
Charred Body (from Chapter 5)
Butcher Knife
Blood (to spurt)
Cunegonde's Jewelry Box with jewels
Wagon
Crust of bread
Meter sticks

CHAPTER EIGHT: AT SEA, TO ARGENTINA
Character Sign: Flashback Old Woman (from Chapter Six)
Scene Sign: "Scene One: James the Anabaptist performs acts of charity, and they talk a lot"
Scene Sign: "Scene Two: Candid pays a visit to Seignor Pococirante, a Noble pessimist, and they talk a lot"
Scene Sign: "Scene Three: Candide has supper with six former heads of state, and they talk a lot"
Scene Sign: "Scene Four: Naked girls being chased by monkeys"

ACT II
PROLOGUE: IN THE JUNGLE (MONKEYS CHASING WOMEN)
Pink ribbons
Two Monkey masks
Rifle for monkey hunting
Weapons for horses
Knife for cutting buttock

CHAPTER NINE: BUENOS AIRES
Pistol
Cartoon Boat (may be same as Chapter Four)
Jewelry Box (from Chapter Seven)

CHAPTER TEN: THE JUNGLE OF PARAGUAY
Plastic Weapons for Revolutionaries
Sword to kill Heinrich

CHAPTER ELEVEN: EL DORADO
Golden ball
Brightly colored paper jewels (to excess)
Pink ribbons for the sheep (all sheep are pink in El Dorado)
A large jewel to bribe Cunegonde
Two Flashlights
Apple (from Chapter One)
Lattè
Dirt from shoes
Pebble from shoe
Sword
Money bag
Guns for Inspector General and Viceroy
Special Effects Bullet
A large paper diamond

CHAPTER TWELVE: THE LAWLESS PORT OF SURINAME
A flogging whip (from Chapter Five)
Severed hand for Pangloss
Severed arm (more of Pangloss)
Layers of jewels for Cunegonde (may be same as Chapter Six jewels)
Cartoonish Pirate Ship (may be same as Chapter Four)
Jolly Roger flag
More paper jewels

CHAPTER THIRTEEN: AT SEA, TO FRANCE
Long strips of blue material for waves

CHAPTER THIRTEEN AND A HALF: PARIS, FRANCE
Wrist watches
Postcards
Diamond Ring (paper diamond)
Garter for the Madame's leg
Letter from Cunegonde
Curtain on pole to obscure Candide's mugging
Police clubs to beat Candide
Character Sign: Flashback Don Fernando...
Character Sign: Flashback Cacambo

CHAPTER FOURTEEN: THE EPILOGUE
An Apple (from Chapter One)
Weapons for final battle

LIST OF CHARACTERS PER SCENE

All cast members appear in Act I Prologue, Chapter 2 for the war, and Chapter 14 for the finale. Additional crowd scenes need all hands on deck in Chapter 5 for the earthquake and Auto-da-fe, Chapter 6 for the Flashback Bulgarian Army, Chapter 7 for the Women Soldiers, Chapter 9 for Townspeople, Chapter 10 for Revolutionary Comrades, Chapter 12 for the Slave Auction, Chapter 13 for dead floating bodies, and Chapter 13½ for vile townspeople.

ACT I PROLOGUE
Baron
Baroness
Paquette
Pangloss
Old Woman
Voltaire
Ben Franklin
All Cast

CHAPTER ONE: WESTPHALIA
Pangloss
Paquette
Old Woman
Baron
Baroness
Candide
Cacambo
Cunegonde
Heinrich
Sheep (four)

CHAPTER TWO: BULGARIA, OR THEREABOUTS
Old Woman
Pangloss
Paquette
Candide
Cacambo
Bulgarian Soldier 1
Bulgarian Soldier 2
Army Deserter
Bulagarian Soldiers
Baron
Baroness
Heinrich
Cunegonde
Sheep

CHAPTER THREE: THE BATTLEFIELD
Pangloss
Candide
Cacambo
Bulgarian Soldier 1
Paquette
A Monk
The Madame
The Pirate Skipper
The Amazon Queen
Christopher Columbus
A Sheep

CHAPTER FOUR: AT SEA, TO PORTUGAL
James the Anabaptist
Pangloss
Candide
Cacambo

CHAPTER FIVE: PORTUGAL
Paquette
Candide
Cacambo
Pnagloss
Townspeople
Inspector General
Executioner 1
Executioner 2
Grand Inquisitor
Viceroy
Biscayan
The Hot Godmother
The Merchant who hates Bacon
Old Woman
Cunegonde

CHAPTER SIX: CUNEGONDE'S HIDEAWAY
Old Woman
Candide
Cunegonde
Paquette
Flashback Cunegonde
Bulgarian Army
Flashback Heinrich
Flashback Baron

Flashback Bulgarian Captain
Flashback Don Issachar
Flashback Old Woman
Flashback Paquette
Flashback Grand Inquisitor
Don Issachar
Grand Inquisitor
Cacambo

CHAPTER SEVEN: THE ROAD TO CADIZ

Pangloss
Executioner 1
Executioner 2
Surgeon
Paquette
Candide
Cunegonde
Cacambo
Old Woman
Horses (two)
Lucky Nun
Unlucky Beggar
Inspector General
Viceroy
Don Issachar
Grand Inquisitor
Drill Sergeant
Woman Soldiers

CHAPTER EIGHT: AT SEA, TO ARGENTINA

Pangloss
Candide
Cunegonde
Old Woman
Cacambo
Paquette
Horses
Sheep (four)
Flashback Old Woman

ACT II PROLOGUE: THE JUNGLE

Old Woman
Eunuch

Paquette
Sheep
Horses
Cannibal 1
Cannibal 2
Cannibal 3
Candide
Cunegonde
Cacambo

CHAPTER NINE: BUENOS AIRES
Paquette
Sexy Woman 1
Sexy Woman 2
Don Fernando
Messenger
Candide
Cunegonde
Old Woman
Cacambo
Sergeant
Horses
Inspector General
Viceroy
Townspeople

CHAPTER TEN: THE JUNGLE OF PARAGUAY
Candide
Cacambo
Paquette
Revolutionary 1
Revolutionary 2
Revolutionary Comrades
Heinrich

CHAPTER ELEVEN: EL DORADO
Old Woman
Paquette
Candide
Cacambo
Amazon Princess 1
Amazon Princess 2
Amazon Queen
Sheep
Don Fernando

Cunegonde
Inspector General
Viceroy
Horses

CHAPTER TWELVE: THE LAWLESS PORT OF SURINAME
Auctioneer
Pangloss
Townspeople
Heinrich
Slave Buyer
Pirate Skipper
Candide
Cacambo
Cunegonde
Paquette
Old Woman
Sheep (two)
Martin the Pessimist

CHAPTER THIRTEEN: AT SEA, TO FRANCE
Old Woman
Martin
Candide
Paquette
Pirate Skipper
Sheep
Pangloss
Heinrich
Dead Bodies

CHAPTER THIRTEEN-AND-A-HALF: PARIS, FRANCE
Old Woman
Martin
Heinrich
Rattoli
Pangloss
Candide
The Madame
Policeman 1
Policeman 2
Mimi
Youyou
Flashback Cunegonde
Sheep

Paquette
Flashback Don Fernando
Flashback Cacambo
Flashback Paquette
Flashback Old Woman
Cacambo
Cunegonde

CHAPTER FOURTEEN: IN CONCLUSION
Candide
Cunegonde
Old Woman
Cacambo
Pangloss
Paquette
Heinrich
Martin
Inspector General
Viceroy
Entire Cast